PERISHED BY A PAINTING

(A Lacey Doyle Cozy Mystery—Book Six)

FIONA GRACE

Fiona Grace

Debut author Fiona Grace is author of the LACEY DOYLE COZY MYSTERY series, comprising nine books (and counting); of the TUSCAN VINEYARD COZY MYSTERY series, comprising six books (and counting); of the DUBIOUS WITCH COZY MYSTERY series, comprising three books (and counting); of the BEACHFRONT BAKERY COZY MYSTERY series, comprising six books (and counting); and of the CATS AND DOGS COZY MYSTERY series, comprising three books (and counting).

Fiona would love to hear from you, so please visit www.fionagraceauthor.com to receive free ebooks, hear the latest news, and stay in touch.

CHAPTER ONE

The smell of roasted tomatoes filled the kitchen of Crag Cottage. Lacey went over to the Aga and retrieved the baking tray. The tomatoes were just starting to caramelize.

"They're done," she announced to Gina.

Her frizzy-gray-haired friend lifted her nose to the air and sniffed. It was the exact same gesture as the two English Shepherd dogs lounging at her feet, and Lacey couldn't help but chuckle.

"That smells wonderful," Gina said.

Lacey smiled nostalgically. "Dad used to make roasted tomato soup on the first day of fall."

Lacey had very few memories of her father. He'd gone missing when she was just a child. But the smell of his roasted tomato soup was as vivid now as ever.

"Good thing I had a kilo's worth of tomatoes left over from the summer then," Gina replied. She adjusted her thick, red-framed glasses and peered out the window at the glorious sunshine. "Hard to believe it's autumn."

It was unseasonably warm, hotter in fact than it had been during the summer. Rays of sun beamed through the big kitchen windows onto Lacey as she went about preparing the soup. She tipped the roasted tomatoes into a big cooking pot, added chicken stock, popped in a few fresh bay leaves from the garden, and set it to simmer. Then she picked up her glass of wine and slid onto a stool opposite Gina at the kitchen island.

"What do you think about sweet peas?" Gina said, peering up from her gardening magazine with her querying blue eyes.

Lacey tucked a dark curl behind her ear and grimaced. "Peas are one of my least favorite vegetables."

Gina laughed. "I don't mean the food! I mean the flowers! For the wedding! It's been weeks since Tom proposed and the only decision you've made so far is putting me in charge of the floral arrangements!"

She was right. It had been weeks since that magical moment when Tom had proposed to Lacey at her surprise fortieth birthday party, and appointing her green-thumbed friend as maid of honor was the only

1

decision she'd actually made. She hadn't even come close to making any arrangements regarding the date, the venue, the dress. Not even the guest list…

And that was the real reason for her hesitance. How could she really plan her dream wedding if her father wasn't there to give her away?

"Show me the picture," she said, trying not to let her sorrow show on her face.

Gina swiveled her magazine around.

Lacey peered at the photograph of delicate little flowers, in a range of pastel-colored pinks, purples, and creams.

"They're a bit… twee," she said.

Gina rolled her eyes to the ceiling. "Do you know you've had something negative to say about every single flower I've suggested so far?"

"I have?" Lacey asked, wincing.

Gina turned the magazine back around. With a shake of the head, she murmured, "I never took you for a Bridezilla."

Of course, Lacey was nothing of the sort. When it came to the particulars of the actual wedding ceremony, she was more relaxed than the average bride-to-be. But she just couldn't face telling Gina that all the flowers in the world couldn't make up for her absent father.

"I'm not being a Bridezilla," she said. "The flowers are just really important to me. More important than anything else. I don't want to rush into any decisions that I might regret later on."

For a brief moment, it looked as if Gina might accept Lacey's explanation. But then she leaned forward on her elbows and narrowed her eyes suspiciously.

"That's not it," she said, like some kind of mind-reading clairvoyant. "I know you too well. What are you hiding, missy?"

"Nothing," Lacey said, defensively, shaking her head.

But she knew Gina wasn't going to drop it. Her friend wasn't one to back away from conflict.

"Oh really?" Gina pressed. "Because you've done next to no planning. You haven't set a date. You shoot down every flower idea I suggest. Dare I say it, but you don't seem that enthusiastic about the wedding."

Lacey let out a scoffing noise of offense.

"I AM enthusiastic," she countered. "I'm just… busy."

"Busy with what?" Gina queried. "The summer tourist period is over. You just hired Finnbar to cover shifts at the store. You've got more time on your hands to plan this wedding than you've had since you left New York!" Her voice softened. She reached out and patted Lacey's hand. "Is it because it's your second wedding? Are you worried it will end badly like last time?"

"It's not that, it's…"

Lacey's explanation was on the tip of her tongue. But she couldn't find the words. They seemed stuck in her mouth like peanut butter. She just couldn't admit to Gina that a couple of weeks back, she'd finally taken the plunge in her attempts to contact her father.

It had all started when she'd gotten a lead on her father from a contact in the antiques world, Jonty Sawyer of Sawyer & Sons Auction House in Weymouth, a place her father had apparently visited every weekend for a year. Jonty had passed on her father's address in England—Mermaid Street in Rye, East Sussex—which Lacey had written down before cowardly stashing it away in a drawer. Like Edgar Allan Poe's tell-tale heart thumping under the floorboards, the drawer seemed to beat at her every time she passed it, forcing her to ruminate over the address hidden inside every second of every minute of every day.

In the end (and with thanks to some Dutch courage), Lacey had managed to pen a letter; an invite to her wedding. Her hope was that her dad might be tempted out of hibernation for her wedding. But she'd received no reply.

The whole thing had left her feeling foolish. What made her think she could entice her father back into her life with a wedding? He'd missed her first wedding to David, after all, so why had she even allowed herself to hope it would be different this time around?

A heaviness settled in Lacey's chest. She decided it would be easier to let Gina think what she wanted.

"You're right," she said, surrendering with a sigh. "That's why I'm dragging my heels."

Gina tutted and shook her head of gray frizz.

"Dear, dear, dear," she said, gently. "What you have with Tom is special. He'd never treat you the way David did, like some kind of incubator for a baby."

Lacey tried to smile, but Gina's clumsy attempt to comfort her had actually dragged up another one of Lacey's biggest insecurities. Having just turned forty, Lacey's window of opportunity for starting her own family was fast running out, and she'd still not made her mind up either way, let alone discussed it with Tom.

3

"Besides," Gina continued, completely oblivious to Lacey's discomfort, "just think how great it will be when your mom and sister and little Frankie come over!"

Far from bolstering her, the thought of her family back home in New York City made Lacey's stomach plummet with shame. Because she hadn't even told them about the engagement yet. Weeks had passed, and everyone from the postman to the milkman knew about Lacey and Tom's engagement. But she'd left her own flesh and blood completely in the dark.

Lacey knew not telling them was unforgivable, no matter how many times she'd tried to rationalize her actions—that she was entitled to her privacy; that she wanted to enjoy the moment with Tom a little longer; that she didn't trust them not to immediately tell her ex-husband and she wanted to avoid talking to him about it for as long as possible—but no matter what excuse she came up with, it was never adequate enough to justify her behavior. There were no two ways about it. By not telling them, she was being a bad daughter, a bad sister, and a bad aunt.

Lacey shifted uncomfortably on her stool and took a deep glug from her wine glass. In response to her silence, Gina gasped.

"You haven't even told them yet," she exclaimed.

She's getting too good at this mind reading malarky, Lacey thought.

"No," she confirmed.

Gina looked horrified. "Why ever not?" she pressed.

Why ever not? Why ever not? The question had been plaguing Lacey just as much as that darn address hidden in her drawer.

Suddenly, Lacey realized all at once that the two were completely connected. The true reason she'd been keeping her engagement a secret was because she was still waiting and hoping that her father would respond to her letter. She was hanging on to that slim possibility, however foolishly, that her wedding may well be the family reunion she'd wanted ever since he'd abandoned her a child. She was waiting on an RSVP she knew would probably never come.

"Well?" Gina prodded.

Just then, the timer in the kitchen started beeping.

"Oops," Lacey said, hopping off her stool. "The soup's ready."

Saved by the bell, she thought as she scurried away from Gina and all her prying questions.

4

CHAPTER TWO

Lacey was busy dusting the shelves of her antiques store when the bell above the door tinkled. Chester let out a bark of excitement, and Lacey glanced over to see Finnbar, her new employee, entering the store.

The skinny young man was wearing the same clothes he did every day: plaid shirt, baggy beige cargo pants, battered leather brogues. His brown hair was an unkempt mess, as was his chin, which was sprouting an array of brown and ginger hairs too long to be stubble but too short to be a beard, as if he couldn't work out which he wanted. Although, knowing how much of a klutz Finnbar had shown himself to be, perhaps he just couldn't work out which way up to hold a razor.

"Good morning," Lacey called.

Finnbar tipped his head in a polite acknowledgment (even though he wasn't wearing a cap), then petted Chester.

"Shall I make a pot of tea?" he asked.

"Please," Lacey said. "All this dusting has left me parched."

She watched Finnbar disappear through the arch to the kitchenette. He was a creature of habit, she noted, always in the same clothes, always starting the day with a head-tip, a pat for Chester, and the offer of a fresh pot of tea. Not that Lacey was complaining about being served tea, but he'd proved himself something of a curious fellow ever since she'd hired him a couple weeks back.

She'd just come into some money, after selling an Isidore Bonheur sculpture to a rich Ukrainian businesswoman. Then Tom had proposed shortly after, and Lacey had decided the best way to spend her money was to hire someone to help in the store so she could free up more time for wedding planning. She and Gina had managed everything between the two of them for months and months on end; it was about time the load was lightened.

Finnbar was doing a PhD in History at Exeter University, so he was the perfect person to man the till on the quieter days. It meant he could read his big tomes in the lull between customers, and occasionally chip in with knowledge about the eras of the antiques. So far, he'd earned himself the nickname "fact machine." But despite his encyclopedic knowledge, he had a staggering lack of common sense.

As Finnbar clattered around in the kitchen, the bell over the door went again, this time ushering in the first customer of the day. Lacey turned her attention to the middle-aged woman, whose shiny, dark brown hair hung neatly above the shoulders of her beautifully tailored gray dress.

"Goodness!" the woman exclaimed, fanning her face. "It's a bit hot in here, isn't it?"

Lacey smiled agreeably. "I'm pretty sure it's hotter now than it was in August!"

But rather than join in with Lacey's friendly banter, the woman frowned.

"Well then why don't you get air conditioning?" she complained.

Lacey felt her enthusiasm falter.

"I don't think it's allowed in this old building," she replied.

The terraced stone buildings that made up the majority of Wilfordshire's architecture were notoriously difficult to modernize. Lacey had to share her utilities with Taryn, the boutique owner next door—which was unfortunate, because Taryn seemed to hate her—and every last alteration had to be approved of by the council. Lacey had had her first request for a sign rejected because the type of wood was "not in keeping with the desired aesthetic of the town," for goodness' sake. Installing a loud, metallic AC unit would probably cause a riot!

"You'll drive away the customers," the woman said haughtily. "It's too stuffy. And it makes the dusty smell worse."

Lacey happened to love the dusty smell of antiques. It was another comfort smell to her, just like roasted tomato soup, because she associated it with her father.

"How can I help you today?" Lacey asked, forcing herself to be polite. The rude woman had really rubbed her the wrong way.

"I'm trying to get a golden wedding anniversary gift for my parents," the woman explained. "They were married in the sixties, so I thought you might have one of those old television sets, the ones the whole family would sit around. Do you know the type I mean?"

Before Lacey had a chance to reply, Finnbar returned from the kitchen with the tray, teapot, and mugs.

"I don't suppose you mean the Sony Trinitron KV-1210?" he asked, as he set the tray down on the counter. "The original twelve-inch model released in 1968?"

He pointed over to the display of electronics.

Lacey blinked at him, perplexed. *How did he know that?*

The woman looked over at the display.

"That's the one!" she exclaimed with glee.

She hurried over and bundled the TV into her arms. Lacey could tell by the way she puffed her cheeks that it was much heavier than she'd anticipated.

"Let me help," Lacey said, taking a step toward her.

"No, no, I've got it," the customer said, brushing her aside.

Lacey watched tensely as the woman waddled over to the counter with the heavy TV set then clumsily plonked it next to the boiling hot teapot. This was a recipe for disaster!

"I assume it works," the customer said to Finnbar, her tone suddenly honeyed.

"As well as it did in the sixties," Finnbar joked in return, his hazel eyes glinting.

The woman who'd been so brusque with Lacey laughed heartily at Finnbar. Clearly she'd taken a shine to him.

As Finnbar rang up the purchase, Lacey watched on tentatively. He was clumsy at the best of times, but now he was negotiating a large electronic device beside a steaming pot of boiling water.

"Would you like me to help you take it to your car?" Finnbar asked, handing the woman her credit card back.

"Oh no, I'll be fine," she trilled.

Lacey braced herself as the woman heaved the heavy set up into her arms and began to waddle for the exit.

"What a charming young man," she said to Lacey as she passed.

Then she exited into the bright late September sunshine with a big grin on her face.

As soon as she was gone, Lacey let out her breath. Disaster averted. She turned to Finnbar.

"I'm impressed," she said. "Not only did you make a difficult customer happy, but you knew the specific type of TV she wanted."

Finnbar shrugged like it was no big deal. "It was the most popular model in the sixties."

"Sure," Lacey said. "But it's still impressive that you know that off the top of your head."

"I have a good memory," Finnbar replied, self-consciously rubbing his unevenly stubbled chin.

He tipped up the teapot and poured a cup for Lacey. But as she took it from him, she looked into the mug and noticed there appeared to be nothing inside but hot water. She began to chuckle.

"Are you sure about having a good memory?" she teased.

Finnbar's dark eyebrows drew together with confusion. "Yes. Why?"

"I think you forgot to put any tea bags in the pot!" Lacey revealed.

Finnbar's cheeks flamed red. His gaze darted down to his own mug.

"Oh!" he said, suddenly flustered. "Silly me. I'm so sorry. Gosh. Let me fix it."

He hastily grabbed for Lacey's mug, clearly panicking. Even his ears were blushing.

Lacey felt bad for having teased him. It was the sort of thing she and Gina would laugh about had either of them made the same mistake, but Finnbar was clearly a more sensitive person than they were. She'd need to be more gentle with him in future.

"It's okay," she said reassuringly. "It's no big deal."

"I—I suppose not," he stammered.

He backed away from her, then scurried off to the kitchen to collect the teabags and correct his mistake.

Lacey watched him with even more curiosity. How could someone so knowledgeable lack such common sense?

Just then, Chester started barking again. Lacey looked to the door to see Tom crossing the cobblestone street between their two stores. The autumn sun made the warm undertone of his skin look almost golden. His brown hair was sunkissed from the long, hot summer, with natural blond highlights accentuating his otherwise chestnut-colored hair. He was in great shape for a man in his early forties. Lacey could see the definition of his muscles through his T-shirt even at this distance.

Tom pushed open the door, making the bell tinkle.

"Good morning fiancée!" he called, grinning a pearly-toothed smile.

Lacey beamed.

"Good morning to you, too, fiancé," she replied. "To what do I owe the pleasure?"

Her handsome beau crossed the floor toward her.

"I have a question for you," he said, his pale green eyes suddenly conveying seriousness. "It's a wedding question."

He said it in a cautious tone that made Lacey pause. Tom had been very patient with her lack of planning so far. He seemed to know that she needed to take things one step at a time, which was impressive for Tom, who could sometimes be so unobservant he was practically blind. But of course, there was going to come a point where she'd need to make some concrete decisions, and it seemed to Lacey that perhaps that time had now come.

"What's the question?" she asked, trying to keep her tone light.

"I was wondering about where we're going to have the wedding," Tom said. "Which country, I mean. UK or US? Because obviously it's traditional to have it in the bride's hometown, but I think my extended family could do with a heads-up if that's the case. Some of them aren't particularly well off financially and it might be a lot to ask them to travel all the way to the States."

He looked uncomfortable asking her and Lacey felt lousy for it. Maybe Gina was right. She was coming across like a total Bridezilla because of the burden of the secret she was keeping.

"Say no more," Lacey said, with a shake of the head. "We'll have it in England."

Tom's green eyes sparked with excitement.

"Really?" he asked. Then he hesitated. "You're not just saying that because I told you my family's too poor to travel?"

Lacey touched his arm reassuringly, her pale fingers in stark contrast to his natural honey-hued skin. "I'm not just saying it, I promise. I want it here. England is my home. More so than the US. It would mean a lot to me to hold it here. Most of the people I love are here, anyway. It would only be Mom, Naomi, and Frankie coming from the States, and a couple of old college friends."

Tom exhaled. "Okay. That's a relief. I didn't want to say, but my uncle is a total cheapskate. When my mom and dad got married, he sent them a bill for his travel expenses!"

Lacey was about to ask more about Uncle Cheapskate when she was distracted by movement over Tom's shoulder. An ominous figure was bobbing around outside the window of her store.

Lacey squinted as she tried to identify the person. Then her chest sank. It was Taryn.

The boutique owner from next door was dressed, as usual, in a black minidress. Her jet black hair was styled in a neat asymmetrical bob (the same style Lacey had sported before she'd let it grow out over the summer; a style she still secretly thought Taryn had copied off her).

"What does she want?" Lacey muttered through her teeth, preemptively irritated.

Like a floating corpse, Taryn pushed open the door and waltzed toward her, her shiny black stilettos stabbing dents into the floorboards. Chester growled as she advanced at the pace of a hurricane.

Lacey suspected some kind of admonishment was coming and braced herself for the storm to hit.

But suddenly, Taryn stopped stomping. She'd noticed Tom standing there, and the change in her demeanor was instantaneous. The frown on her wrinkle-free brow smoothed out and a bright (if stilted) smile appeared on her face.

"Thomas!" she exclaimed. "I understand congratulations are in order."

Lacey noticed the way her smile broke as she said it, revealing a brief grimace beneath. Taryn and Tom had dated many moons ago, way before Lacey was on the scene, but the fashionista clearly still held a flame for him. It was obvious that the last thing she wanted to do was congratulate the pair of them.

"Thanks, Taryn," Tom said, oblivious to the undercurrent.

Taryn air kissed his cheeks, then turned to Lacey. "Congratulations to you too, Lacey. You give the rest of us hope."

Ah, the typical Taryn back-handed compliment, Lacey thought.

"Did you want something?" Lacey asked, forcing pleasantness.

"I do," Taryn replied in an efficient businesslike voice. "It won't take long."

Lacey flashed her a skeptical look. Taryn always said "it won't take long" just before she took up all of Lacey's time.

She looked over at Tom. "Excuse me for a second."

He nodded and stepped away, taking out his cell phone. Probably to play the war game he'd become addicted to recently…

Lacey gave her full attention to Taryn. "So what is it?"

"It's about the air conditioning situation," Taryn said. "You know how we can't have external machines. But the place is boiling and my customers are complaining. Standing fans just aren't doing the trick."

"And?" Lacey asked, not sure what any of this had to do with her.

"I've found out about a loophole," Taryn announced triumphantly. "But I need you on board for it to work."

Lacey already didn't like the sound of this.

"What exactly does this loophole involve?" she asked.

Taryn pointed a bony finger toward the alcove on their shared wall. "There's a boarded up chimney breast behind there, and we can have an internal system installed via it. I know a guy who will convert it for us,

10

and since there won't be anything on the outside, we can install it without planning permission and without the council sticking their noses in."

Lacey frowned, skeptical.

"Why do you need me?" she asked.

"That's the thing," Taryn replied. "He'll need to knock through the chimney on both sides."

"Why?"

"Do I look like I work in construction?" Taryn challenged, opening her arms to gesture to her stylish outfit.

Lacey rolled her eyes, her patience waning. "Point taken. Do you know how long it will take, at least? And how much it will cost?"

"Well, I wanted you on board before I bothered getting any quotes," Taryn replied defensively.

"Okay, well, me being on board kinda depends on how much it costs."

Taryn huffed. "I knew you'd be difficult about it!"

"I'm not being difficult," Lacey refuted. "I'm asking questions! It will be disruptive having workmen in here, and I don't know how cost effective it will really be for me. Having an air-conditioned atmosphere is less important to my clientele than to yours."

She thought then of the customer earlier who'd complained about the heat. Maybe it was a good idea, after all?

"Fine," Taryn snapped, cutting Lacey off before she had a chance to give it any more thought. "I'll get a quote and email it to you."

She turned and marched away, completely forgetting to put on her happy-act for Tom's benefit. It didn't matter though; he didn't notice her leave at all. He'd been tapping away on his phone the whole time, clearly completely absorbed with his silly war game.

"How's your infantry coming along?" Lacey called over to him, gently teasing.

Tom's attention darted up from his phone to Lacey. "Actually, I wasn't playing my game. I was texting your mom."

Lacey frowned with curiosity.

"Why?" she queried.

"To make sure she doesn't mind traveling for the wedding," Tom said.

Lacey's stomach dropped. Her mouth fell open.

Oh no. Oh no, no, no!

"Tom!" she cried, panicking. "I haven't told them yet!"

11

"Haven't told them what?" Tom asked, frowning in response to her horrified expression.

"I haven't told my family that we're engaged!" she exclaimed.

The admission hung in the space between them. Then Tom's expression turned aghast.

"What?" he cried.

But before Lacey got a chance to explain herself, her cell phone began to ring. It would be her mom. She just knew it.

She tore her eyes away from Tom and grabbed her phone. Sure enough, the name *Mom* was blinking up at her.

Lacey's stomach flip-flopped. She was in big, big trouble.

CHAPTER THREE

Lacey held her insistently vibrating cell phone out at arm's length. But she knew she couldn't put it off anymore. It was time to face the music.

She knew it was going to be a very awkward conversation and she didn't want Tom overhearing her stuttering her way through it, so she decided to head to the garden for privacy.

She left Tom on the main shop floor looking shell-shocked, and hurried into the auction room, heading for the French doors. At the sound of her rushing past, Finnbar poked his head out of the storeroom and flashed her a bemused look. Lacey didn't stop to explain. She just launched herself through the French doors into the garden and hit the green button.

She listened anxiously as the call connected.

"Hello, Lacey," came her mom's dispassionate voice. "This is your mother. Remember me? I'm the woman who gave you life. Who birthed you."

Lacey inhaled. They were already off to a great start.

"Mom, before you say anything, let me explain," she said, cautiously.

Shirley's calm, cold persona immediately gave way to anger.

"Explain?" she yelled. "There's no way to explain yourself out of this one, Lacey! You're getting married? And you didn't tell me? I had to find out, by accident, from Tom? Who, incidentally, returns my calls and messages in a far more timely manner than you do."

Guilt swirled in Lacey's guts. She grimaced.

"I'm really sorry, Mom," she said. "I wasn't not telling you. I haven't told anybody yet."

It was technically true. Since Tom had proposed in front of everyone at her birthday bash, she hadn't needed to tell anybody because they all already knew. But a technicality wasn't going to spare Lacey from the shame she felt, nor the wrath of her mother scorned.

"So it is true?" Shirley demanded. "You and Tom really are engaged?"

13

Lacey's stomach churned. In a small, apologetic voice, she confirmed it. "Yes. We are."

"I cannot believe you!" Shirley screeched.

Lacey patiently listened to her mother's angry monologue. It was the least she could do considering the way in which her mom had found out.

When Shirley finally fell silent, Lacey took her chance to grovel.

"I'm so sorry, Mom," she said quickly, before Shirley could start her angry tirade anew. "It wasn't my intention to hurt you. I've wanted to tell you, truly, but..." She pictured her letter to her father. Her hand as she pushed it into the mouth of the red mailbox, never to be seen again. "It's too complicated to explain so I won't try. I'll just say sorry and hope you can forgive me."

On the other end of the line, all was silent.

"Mom?" Lacey asked. "Are you still there?"

Still nothing. For a heart-wrenching moment, Lacey thought she might have made her mother cry. But then she heard a series of bleeps on the line and the background hum changed.

Must be a bad connection, Lacey thought.

"Hello?" she tried again. "Are you there?"

"Yes, I'm here," came a voice that was not Shirley's, but Naomi's.

"Naomi?" Lacey asked, shocked. What was her sister doing on the line? "What happened to Mom?"

"I'm here, too," Shirley said.

Suddenly, it dawned on Lacey what was happening; her mom had patched her little sister into the call for backup. Now Lacey would have to grovel to both of them! Naomi was dramatic at the best of times; there was no way she'd hold back on something as big as this!

Lacey tensed with nervous apprehension.

"What's this about?" Naomi asked, sounding confused.

"Tell her, Lacey," Shirley commanded. "Tell her what you've done."

"Oh God..." Naomi said, her confusion immediately giving way to panic. "What have you done?"

"Nothing!" Lacey hurriedly assured her. She fully accepted she was at fault here but her mom had made it sound ominous, like she'd murdered someone! "Well, nothing illegal at least."

"Just spit it out," Naomi snapped. She was never one to mince her words.

"Yes, do come on, Lacey," Shirley added witheringly. "Don't keep your sister in suspense."

Lacey's heart was starting to palpitate. She tugged the collar of her shirt, which seemed suddenly very constricting.

"I—I have some news," she stammered. "Tom proposed. And I said yes."

"Whaaaat?" Naomi squealed. "You're engaged?"

"Surprise," Lacey added meekly.

There was a brief pause before Naomi said, simply, "Wow."

Lacey didn't quite know what to make of her "wow." She was surprised, that much was evident. But whether she was good surprised or bad surprised was nearly impossible to ascertain. And she hadn't even told her the bad bit yet…

"I'm in shock," Naomi murmured. "You're getting married before me. Again. There really must be something wrong with me if you can get married twice before I even walk down the aisle once. But I guess if I rushed into relationships like you do I could've been married a few times by now as well."

Lacey scowled. She should've expected a tactless response like that from her younger sister.

"None of this is the issue," Shirley interjected. "The issue is that Lacey didn't tell us. She wasn't going to tell us at all. I only found out by accident from Tom. Isn't that right, Lacey? Tell her."

Lacey didn't get a chance, because Naomi was already dramatically gasping.

"You weren't going to tell us?" she squealed. "Why on earth not?"

Lacey tried to explain herself, but her voice was drowned out by her sister's. And anyway, what satisfactory answer could she really give? She couldn't exactly drop the bombshell on them that she'd traced their long-lost father and had invited him to the wedding!

"How long have you been hiding it from us?" Naomi demanded. She sounded hurt.

Lacey bit her lip. "Since my birthday."

"That was weeks ago!" Shirley cried, shrilly.

"Oh, Lacey," Naomi said reproachfully.

"Listen to this," Shirley interrupted, sounding very much like she'd stepped onto her soapbox. "*Dear future Mother-in-law. Lacey and I have decided we'd like the wedding to be in the UK. But of course if the travel is a problem for you, we'd be happy to make different arrangements. Your son-in-law-to-be, Tom.*' Can you believe it? Can you imagine finding out about your daughter's wedding from a text message like that?"

"Awful," Naomi said with a disapproving *tsk*. "Just awful."

In any other circumstance, Lacey would've found Tom's message adorably touching. But right now, under the heat of her mom and sister, she really wished he'd not put his foot in it…

Still, the blame was all hers, at the end of the day. She was the one who'd gotten herself into this mess. Her family was highly emotional at the best of times, but she couldn't really fault them for their reactions. She should've told them right off the bat.

She slumped her back against the grubby glass greenhouse door, thinking again of the reason she'd stalled. Her father.

She kicked at a tuft of dry grass growing between the paving slabs as she imagined him reading her letter, then screwing it up and throwing it straight in the trash. Lacey kicked the grass tuft hard enough for it to dislodge from the crack and spray shards of dried dirt across the slab.

"Do you know when you might be having it?" Naomi asked.

Lacey paused. It sounded like they were done bashing her. At least for now.

"Not yet," she said, cautiously. "I haven't made any decisions, apart from making Gina my maid of honor slash chief gardener. But you know fall is my favorite season, but that would mean waiting a full year. Spring would be too soon, summer's already booked up, and winter is out for obvious reasons."

Lacey waited, hopeful that perhaps her mom and sister were done with their admonishments and could celebrate with her.

"Just make sure it's during Frankie's vacation, okay?" Naomi said, with a weary sigh. "He's not allowed out of school during term time and he'd be devastated to miss it."

"Good to know," Lacey replied.

It wasn't exactly a celebratory comment, but at least the disappointed bit was over. And the unpleasant telephone call hadn't been entirely fruitless, Lacey thought, looking on the bright side. At least now she knew to make arrangements around Frankie's term times. There was no way she was getting married without her ginger-haired partner in crime there. In fact, maybe if her dad was out of the question for aisle walking duties, Frankie would want to do it. He was technically the man of the family.

"Did you say you made Gina the maid of honor?" came Naomi's voice in Lacey's ear.

"Yeah," Lacey said, sounding more conversational now she'd allowed her defenses to drop a little. "She's the obvious choice. She's my neighbor, employee, friend, mentor, dog-walking buddy..."

Lacey's voice trailed off as she suddenly realized her mistake. *Naomi* was supposed to be the maid of honor! In a traditional wedding, it was common for the sister of the bride to be given a vital role. Lacey had bumbled straight into another faux pas.

"But really that's not set in stone either," Lacey said hurriedly, trying to make amends. "Her real role is chief gardener."

"Huh," Naomi replied, despondently.

The damage was already done.

After a few more minutes of questions she couldn't answer, Lacey ended the call and slunk back into the store, her shoulders slumped. The telephone call had frayed her nerves so thoroughly she felt like they might snap at any slight provocation. Any more wedding questions and she'd lose it for real.

Tom was still standing in the middle of the room where she'd left him, wearing the same look of horrified guilt as before.

"I am so sorry," he said immediately, pacing toward her.

"Don't be," Lacey said, shaking her head. "It's not your fault. It's mine."

The last thing she needed was for him to feel guilty about letting the cat out of the bag. What was done was done. It was best to just move on.

Tom reached her and wrapped her into a bear hug. Lacey breathed in his comforting buttery scent.

"I didn't mean to make anything difficult for you," Tom said, while bestowing a series of pecks on the crown of her head. "Can I come by the cottage this evening to make you an apology dinner?"

Lacey moved out of the embrace and gave him an earnest look.

"I told you, you don't have to apologize," she said. Then she wiggled her eyebrows cheekily. "But you can still make me dinner."

Tom smirked. "Anything for my beautiful fiancée. What do you want?"

"Something fallish," Lacey suggested.

"Good call," Tom said. "How about roasted tomato soup?"

Lacey's smile widened. "That sounds perfect."

Just then, the sound of papers and books being dropped came from behind. Lacey turned to see Finnbar standing in the archway, surrounded by paper. He must've been eavesdropping.

Tom released her from his embrace.

"I'll leave you to it," he said, wiggling his eyebrows knowingly.

He'd heard plenty about Finnbar's clumsiness over the weeks.

He left the store and Lacey approached Finnbar. The young man looked extremely uncomfortable as he hastily tried to collect his strewn papers and books.

Lacey crouched to help.

"You overheard all that, I take it?" she asked, scraping pages of notes off the floorboards.

"Yeah," he said, awkwardly. "Is everything okay?"

He seemed anxious. Considering the incident had nothing to do with him, his worry seemed overblown.

"With me and Tom?" Lacey said. "Yes, it's fine."

"It sounded like an argument," Finnbar replied.

"Not really," Lacey said. "There's no point in me being mad. It was an honest mix-up."

"I meant the other way round," Finnbar said. "Isn't Tom mad at you?"

His question confused Lacey. Tom had been the one in the wrong, telling her family before she was ready. Why would he be the one who was mad?

"What do you mean?" she asked.

Finnbar shoved his glasses back up the bridge of his nose. "Well, it's just, if I were him, I'd be really hurt that you didn't tell your family about the engagement."

He bundled the rest of his papers in his arms and scurried away.

Lacey sat back on her haunches, pondering Finnbar's words.

What did Tom really think about her withholding the news from her family? Was he upset and hiding it? Had she not even known that she'd hurt her partner's feelings?

She would have to discuss it with him later that night.

CHAPTER FOUR

That evening, Tom arrived on the doorstep of Crag Cottage holding a cardboard box full of vegetables.

"What happened to tomato soup?" Lacey asked, picking up a zucchini and waggling it around.

"Change of plan," Tom said. "I got all this produce for cheap because it's misshapen. I figured I'd make Wonky Courgette Casserole for dinner, if that's okay with you?"

"Of course it is!" Lacey said, giggling at his cute name of the dish and his use of the French term *courgette* instead of zucchini.

Tom bustled inside with his box, negotiating his way through the assault course that was Chester excitedly weaving between his legs. Once he made it to the kitchen without tripping over, he placed the box down on the counter.

"What wine pairs well with zucchini?" Lacey asked, heading for the wine fridge.

Tom was a foodie. Though he'd devoted his life to pastry, his knowledge of food and wine was rather extensive.

"A sauvignon blanc," Tom said as he began laying vegetables on the counter. "Or, failing that, a pinot."

"Is a New Zealand sauvignon okay?" Lacey called, as she retrieved a chilled bottle from the metal wrack and inspected the label.

"Perfect," Tom replied.

Lacey took the cold bottle over to the counter and corkscrewed it open. Then she poured them each a glass and presented one to Tom.

"There you go, fiancé," she said.

Tom put down his chopping knife.

"Thank you, fiancée," he said.

They'd taken to calling one another by the moniker. Before, they hadn't settled on any pet names, fluctuating between *dear* and *love*, but as soon as the ring was on Lacey's finger, they'd automatically taken to calling one another fiancé(e).

Tom clinked his glass against Lacey's.

"A toast to you," he said. "For surviving an extremely awkward telephone conversation with your folks that was all my fault."

19

Lacey chuckled. "To me," she echoed.

She took a sip of wine, and lent against the counter as Tom started to chop. As she watched him, her ruminations about Finnbar's question from earlier came back to her. She bit down on her lip with apprehension.

"Are you upset that I didn't tell my family about the engagement?" she asked.

Tom didn't even look up from his zucchini slicing.

"Not at all," he said.

"So it didn't make you feel bad when you found out I'd not told them?" Lacey pressed.

"Why would it?" Tom replied.

He sounded distinctly like he was only half listening. Which was fair enough. Multi-tasking wasn't exactly Tom's forte.

Lacey tried a different approach. "How did you feel when you found out I hadn't told them yet?"

Tom didn't even slow his chopping pace, which was exceptionally fast. "Guilty. For accidentally telling them when you obviously weren't ready."

Lacey took another sip of wine. She wasn't quite buying it, and not just because Tom was clearly only giving her fifty percent of his attention. He could insist it didn't bother him until the cows came home, but Lacey would still have a niggle of a doubt.

"Did you tell Heidi right away?" she asked.

Lacey had only met Tom's lawyer mom on a handful of occasions, and the first had been while sitting in the Wilfordshire police station having been arrested and falsely accused of murder. Ever since then, Lacey felt like she was playing catch-up when it came to getting her future mother-in-law to like her.

"I told her the day after," Tom said. "And then I called Norah and told her later that evening."

Lacey frowned. Who was Norah? She'd not heard the name before and was hesitant to ask.

"Who's Norah?" she said, eventually.

"My sister," Tom said, simply.

Lacey almost spit her wine out. "You have a SISTER?"

Her exclamation was enough to finally tear Tom's attention away from his task. He looked at her, surprised.

"Yes…" he said, drawing out the word like it was a question. "My older sister. Norah. You know I have a sister, don't you?"

"No!" Lacey squealed.

She was completely floored. Had he told her and she'd forgotten? Surely not! Surely she wouldn't have forgotten something as important as a sister? Especially since she was always dealing with her own sister-related drama. It would've been something for them to bond over if she'd known anything about it.

"Well, we're not really that close," Tom said, flippantly, as if that was an even remotely adequate explanation for the gaping gap in Lacey's knowledge. "I mean, if you want to get technical, she's not actually my sister at all. We don't even share any genes."

"What do you mean, you don't share any jeans?" Lacey questioned. "What's that got to do with anything? It would be super weird if you did, to be honest. Women's jeans are cut completely differently and—"

Tom cut her off with a bark of laughter.

"GENES!" he cried. "G-E-N-E-S."

"Oh."

Lacey felt foolish. Her cheeks became warm. But when she realized what Tom was actually saying, her embarrassment gave way to utter confusion.

"Wait one second," she said, seeking clarification. "You don't share genes? So you're not actually related?"

She couldn't cope with this back and forth, up and down, in and out topsy-turviness. She would very much like to get off the emotional rollercoaster Tom's shocking revelation had forced her onto.

Tom looked like he was trying to solve a very tricky math puzzle.

"She's my *step*sister," he said with consideration, as if this was the first time he'd tried to make sense of it. "Sort of. She's from my dad's previous marriage, his first wife's daughter, his stepdaughter. Which would technically make her my stepsister, only my dad and her mom divorced before I was born. So she's kinda like my ex-stepsister. OR… my never stepsister?"

Lacey blinked. Tom's family history was perplexing to say the least. But the fact Lacey knew so little of it was the real issue.

"You know another term for a never stepsister?" she said.

"No? What?" Tom replied.

"Just nothing," Lacey said, with a shrug. "You just call her Norah, and I don't have a heart attack."

Tom laughed, though Lacey was really only half joking.

"But that wouldn't be right either," he explained. "Norah lived with my dad and his first wife for most of her childhood. He was basically a second father to her, and they stayed close even after the divorce. I remember her calling me her brother when I was younger, but I guess after Dad died we just drifted apart. There's a huge age gap between us, so it's bound to happen." He lowered his voice and stage-whispered as if he was revealing something scandalous. "She's only a couple years younger than my mom."

And with that, he blithely went back to chopping his zucchinis.

Lacey stood there, completely floored. She had known about precisely none of this. Tom wasn't exactly guarded about his family (although he struggled to discuss his father, who'd passed away when he was young), and yet Lacey knew nothing about Heidi being Tom's dad's second wife, and she certainly knew nothing about Norah, his sort-of not-quite stepsister! However tangential the relation actually was between Tom and Norah, surely she would've come up in conversation at least once during the course of their relationship.

"You never told me any of that before," Lacey murmured, feeling insecure.

Tom just shrugged. "Oh well. Now you know."

He was being typically glib.

"Not 'oh well,'" Lacey countered. "Why have you never talked about Norah before? Or your dad's first marriage? Why am I only just finding out about it now?"

Tom paused mid-chop. He turned to her, his chestnut brows furrowed in question.

"You're stressing, aren't you?" he said, finally picking up on her emotional state. "Why is this bothering you so much?"

Lacey shook her head. She didn't fully understand herself. But she had an inkling...

"I wrote a letter to my dad," she blurted.

Several beats of silence passed.

Finally, Tom's eyes widened. He placed his knife down clumsily.

"Really?" he exclaimed. "You found an address for him?"

Lacey nodded. Her heart was hammering like a pneumatic drill. "I met someone at the Sawyer & Sons auction house who knew him. They had an address. He lives in Rye, in Sussex."

As it all came pouring out, Lacey felt like a huge weight was lifting from her shoulders. She hadn't realized just how much her secret had been weighing on her. She felt foolish for having hidden it in the first place.

"Lacey, this is incredible!" Tom exclaimed. "We should go there. Together."

"What?" Lacey said, taken aback. "No. We can't do that."

"Why not?" Tom pressed. "You finally know where your dad lives! After all that searching. Don't you want to go and see him?"

Lacey balked.

"Of course," she mumbled. Her gaze fell to the stem of her wine glass which she'd begun nervously twiddling in her fingers. "But he hasn't replied to my letter. So I don't know if he... you know..." Her voice dropped even lower, "...wants to see me."

"Ah," Tom said, turning instantly serious.

He reached for her and took her in his arms. Lacey accepted the comfort.

"Here's an idea," he said. "Why don't we go together? Make a weekend of it?"

"No way," Lacey said, shaking her head against his chest. "It took me weeks just to write him a letter. I'm hardly ready to knock on his door."

Tom released her from his embrace. "Then how about we just look at his house from afar?"

"No," Lacey said more firmly. "I'm sorry, Tom, but I'm just not ready."

"Visit the town?" Tom suggested. "The county?"

He was getting farther and farther away and Lacey couldn't help but feel touched by his efforts to encourage her, even if he was being a bit pushy about it.

"I'll visit the county," Lacey said, relenting. "That's as close as I'm comfortable getting. For now."

Tom clapped his hands triumphantly. "Excellent! We're well overdue a trip and there are tons of awesome beach towns on the Sussex coast. And this time, it'll be just the two of us, without your family!"

He wiggled his brows in reference to his last transgression.

Lacey chuckled.

"You're talking about it like it's going to happen," she said.

"Because it is," Tom replied.

Lacey shook her head. "We can't go on a trip. We have no free time. We've both got tons of work stuff coming up, what with Halloween just around the corner."

23

"You're right," Tom said. Then he flashed her a mischievous grin. "Unless we go tomorrow?"

Now he was talking crazy! They couldn't just spontaneously take to the road. They had businesses to run. Appointments to keep. Besides, the last time Lacey had done something spontaneous, she'd ended up quitting her job and moving to a different country!

"We can't go tomorrow," Lacey said, shaking her head.

But Tom wasn't backing down. "Why not? Let's just pack a bag and take to the road! Explore the Sussex coast for a few days. I have Emmanuel at the patisserie and you have Finnbar and Gina at the store, there's really no reason not to."

Lacey hesitated. Maybe Tom was right. This weekend was their last chance to get away before they got super busy again preparing for Halloween. If not now, then when?

"Okay," she blurted, surprising herself. "Let's do it."

"Really?" Tom exclaimed. His smile widened to the gorgeous kilowatt grin that had swept Lacey off her feet all those months ago.

"Yes. Really," she said. "Let's pack a bag and hit the road. Why not?" Excitement crackled through her veins. "What's the worst that could happen?"

CHAPTER FIVE

"This is the number for the security firm," Lacey said to Finnbar, pointing at the pinboard in her office. It was covered in several overlapping layers of colored sticky notes. "If the alarm gets triggered accidentally, you need to call them within thirty seconds and give them this passcode." She tapped the pink sticky note. "Otherwise they'll think you're a burglar and I'll have to pay a fee for them to reset the system. Got it?"

Finnbar glanced up from his notebook. "Got it."

It was the morning after Tom's idea for a spontaneous road trip and Lacey's mood had turned from giddy excitement to extreme nervousness about leaving her store in the hands of ditzy Gina and klutzy Finnbar. Luckily, it hadn't taken much to convince Tom to agree to stop by their respective stores before they took to the wind; he knew she'd be anxious the whole weekend otherwise.

"I think that's everything," Lacey said to Finnbar. "Unless you can think of anything else? You know you have to keep receipts for the petty cash tin? And that the combination for the lock box is next to the till? And you know where the coffee pods are kept...?"

She was fretting now, she knew. But leaving the store was hard for Lacey. She imagined it felt a bit like when a mom left their newborn for the first time.

Finnbar shut his notebook. He had enough notes to write a whole PhD on how to run the store.

"We've covered everything," he said with a decisive nod.

Lacey chewed her lip apprehensively as they exited through the office door. She wasn't convinced.

"If you have any questions you can always ask Gina," she told him, continuing her anxious explanations. "And if you have any questions about Gina, ring me."

Finnbar smirked. "Got it."

They entered the main shop floor. Gina looked over with suspiciously narrowed eyes. She'd made it quite clear she was opposed to Lacey's impromptu trip, not because she didn't want her friend to get

25

the romantic getaway she deserved, but because she wasn't convinced about Finnbar's employment at the store in general.

As Finnbar went over to the shelves to dust the pottery, Gina sidled up to Lacey.

"Did you give him the passcode?" she said under her breath.

"Yes."

"Are you sure that's a good idea?"

"Why wouldn't it be?" Lacey replied.

"Because he might do something with it," Gina whispered.

"Like what?" Lacey challenged. "The only thing he can do is save me from getting a fine if the alarm gets tripped accidentally."

"He could be a burglar," Gina said, conspiratorially.

"He's playing a very long game if he is," Lacey replied. "And giving him the passcode for the security system isn't going to stop him burglarizing us if that's what he wants to do. He has a set of keys."

"He does?" Gina exclaimed. "Since when?"

"Since last week," Lacey said. She shook her head. Gina's paranoia was only making her more apprehensive. "You should be glad. It means when I'm away, someone else can lock up. You know how much you hate doing it."

"Only because I hate the responsibility of knowing that if something goes wrong, the buck stops with me. Having him do it doesn't make that better, does it? The buck still stops with me as his supervisor. I'll probably end up walking over here in the middle of the night to check all the locks now."

"Well then that will give you a chance to water the garden under the moonlight, just like you love to do."

"Lacey," Gina said with a frown.

"Gina," Lacey said, firmly. "Please stop. I'm worried enough as it is about leaving the store. The last thing I need is for you to stress me out even more."

"All right, all right," Gina said, finally relenting. "You deserve to relax."

"Thank you," Lacey said.

Just then, an enormous crash sounded. The two women looked up. Finnbar was standing with his feather duster poised and shards of porcelain at his feet. He'd knocked a vase off the shelf.

"I'm so sorry!" he exclaimed.

Gina clapped a hand down on Lacey's shoulder.

"See! We've got everything here covered," she joked.

Lacey nerves frayed. She got the distinct feeling she'd be returning to a catastrophe.

*

Lacey felt a mixture of excitement and guilt as she left her store and headed around the street corner. Excited because they were well overdue a redo of their earlier disastrous trip to Dover, but guilty for leaving her store at such short notice.

She headed to where Tom's van was parked around the corner. They'd decided it would be more comfortable to travel in his van than in Lacey's unreliable secondhand car, especially as it gave Chester plenty of room to spread out in the back seat.

Lacey hopped in and glanced over her shoulder at her trusty pooch. He was already snoozing, wedged in beside two large cardboard boxes.

"What are those?" Lacey asked Tom.

When they'd packed this morning, all they'd had was a hold-all of clothes each, and a backpack in case of any hiking opportunities. Now the back seat looked like they were moving across states.

In the driver's seat, Tom turned to her and grinned. "While you were in your shop, I went into mine and collected some stuff from the storeroom."

He said it innocently enough, but Lacey narrowed her eyes with skepticism. Tom had an adventurous streak that Lacey didn't share. If there was a tent back there she may as well get out now and go back to work. There was no way this spontaneous romantic trip was going to turn into a camping one.

"What stuff?" she asked suspiciously.

"Just stuff," Tom said again, evasively.

"Tom…" Lacey warned.

"It's an inflatable dinghy," he said. "And a couple of paddleboards."

Lacey exhaled. She shook her head. "You know I'm not going to use them. They're just taking up space."

"They're there in case the mood strikes," Tom said, with a cheeky grin.

"Sure," Lacey replied dryly. "This weekend, out of forty years' worth of weekends, will be the one where the mood suddenly strikes me to take up water sports."

Tom chuckled. "You never know."

He turned the key in the ignition and the van rumbled to life. Lacey felt a ripple of emotion run through her. She was excited to be getting away from it all. But she was also nervous about knowing she'd be closing the distance between herself and her father, and that if she chose to, she could close that distance completely for the first time since she was seven years old, by knocking on his door.

Tom pulled away from the curb and joined the stream of cars heading out of Wilfordshire, taking the A road heading east. The plan was to take the coast route to Sussex, and stop off at any town they liked the look of. Lacey wanted to see Brighton, a trendy coastal city filled with Regency, Edwardian, and Art Deco architecture. It sounded like just the sort of place she loved, so she was planning on keeping her lips shut until they reached it.

"Have you really never done water sports?" Tom asked her as he drove.

"Nope," Lacey replied. "I haven't bungee jumped or rappelled down a mountain or jumped out of a plane either."

"Really?" Tom said, sounding surprised. "I've done all three. More than once."

"I just don't see the point. When will it ever be useful in my life to know how to, I dunno, rock climb or whatever?" She shrugged. "But I guess I'm not very adventurous. All I ever cared about was doing well at school and getting a good job. Two crazy, unstable parents will do that to a girl."

She fell quiet, not wanting to think about her father and how he'd failed to respond to her letter.

"I have an idea," Tom said. "Let's play Would You Rather. I'll start. Would you rather bungee jump or abseil—or rappel, as you Americans call it?"

Lacey rolled her eyes. "Neither."

"That's not how the game works," Tom told her. "You have to answer."

"Fine. Rappel. Would you rather have four legs or four arms?"

Tom laughed heartily. "That took a turn for the surreal."

"Well?" Lacey prompted.

"Arms. Think how many cakes I could make with four arms! I'd double my output. Then double my income. Then buy you a beautiful seaside house, where we could paddleboard to our hearts' content."

Lacey looked over at her handsome beau. "Seaside house?" she queried.

"Sure," he said, breezily. "Isn't that everyone's fantasy?"

Lacey hadn't given any thought to where they would live after they tied the knot. She'd just assumed Tom would move into her cottage on the cliffs. But it sounded like he had other plans. If he wanted them to buy a house together, would she have to sell her dream home?

She added it to her list of unknowns. It seemed to be growing quite rapidly. She didn't know if she'd take Tom's surname. She didn't know if she'd have Tom's babies. And now she didn't even know where she and Tom would live.

Suddenly, Lacey recalled Naomi's insinuation during her phone call that she was rushing into her marriage with Tom.

For the first time, Lacey began to worry that maybe she was.

CHAPTER SIX

Brighton was an interesting town, with peppermint-green railings and a steep rocky cliff dropping down to a beach filled with pebbles. Despite the discomfort Lacey would expect from sitting on a pebbly beach, it was completely packed, with groups of people sitting almost shoulder to shoulder. And she'd thought Bournemouth was busy...

The architecture of Brighton was also amazing. Mile after mile of the coast was taken up by huge, terraced town houses in a Regency style. They were the sort of houses Lacey imagined the characters from Jane Austen novels living in. Their facades were painted white, but the paint was peeling in places and grimy from rain and pollution. It gave Brighton the feel of fading grandeur, something Lacey couldn't help but find impossibly romantic.

Between the houses was a four-lane road for cars, plus a separate bus lane. Then there was a wide pavement with a cycle lane, which was also filled with skateboarders and rollerbladers. Next to that was a large swath of grass filled with dog walkers and Frisbee throwers, and rows upon rows of brightly painted beach huts separating the lawns from the pebbly beach.

Chester sniffed through the open crack in the window, wagging his tail with excitement.

"How set are you on a seaside house?" Lacey asked Tom, as she craned her head to look out the window. "Because Brighton is looking very appealing right about now."

"Appealing," Tom agreed. "But very expensive. You know all these houses are owned by famous people?" He pointed at the Regency period houses Lacey had been admiring.

"Really?" she asked. "Like who?"

Before Tom got a chance to reveal any names, Lacey's attention was suddenly diverted to a palace-like building. It could only be described as a mini Taj Mahal, with domes and minarets, and a garden surrounding it filled with trees and flowers.

"Look at that!" Lacey cried with excitement. "Tom! Look!"

He peered across the steering wheel. "That's the Royal Pavilion. It was built by King George. Brighton used to be the royal family's favorite seaside retreat."

"Is it still owned by the royals?"

"No, it's a museum and venue now. You can get married there."

"Really?" Lacey squealed. Now she was getting ideas...

"Want to look?" Tom said.

"Yes, please!" Lacey exclaimed.

They parked the van in an underground lot nearby, then walked back to the Royal Pavilion. They entered into the garden from the back entrance, which was open to the public. The lawn was full of people hanging out, and there was a little café with bistro tables filled with people eating sandwiches while swatting away seagulls. Chester bolted straight at the birds, sending them flying into the air in a flurry of feathers.

Lacey let her imagination run wild, picturing the whole place filled with her wedding party, with her in a white dress having photographs taken outside the spectacular castle.

They headed inside and Lacey gaped at the crazy technicolor decor. Huge chandeliers hung from the ceiling, which was domed and painted bright blue. Red velvet curtains fringed with gold thread hung over the large windows, matching the red rug that ran along the length of the room like they were at a Hollywood premiere. There were statues and suits of armor everywhere.

"King George had an eclectic taste," Lacey commented, as she glanced around at the bright, gaudy wallpaper and decadent furniture.

Tom chuckled. "You're getting ideas, aren't you?"

"Maybe..." Lacey confessed.

It would be totally over the top to hold their wedding in such a place. But Lacey was so understated usually, maybe her wedding should be a huge extravaganza?

After looking around the palace, Tom and Lacey decided it was time for lunch.

"I know the best place," Tom said.

He guided Lacey and Chester into a narrow road crammed with shops, street stalls, and people walking shoulder to shoulder. Brighton seemed to have an abundance of eateries, from cool cafés to fancy restaurants. At least fifty percent of them were exclusively vegetarian or vegan cuisine, which suited Lacey just fine for lunch; she had a hankering for something fresh.

Tom directed Lacey up a rickety wooden staircase into a tiny little canteen-style café, with bistro tables on a balcony overhanging the street below. It was the perfect spot for people watching, Lacey thought as she settled into her seat.

Chester curled up under the table while Lacey perused the menu. Everything on sale was organic, locally produced, and exceptionally tasty sounding. She chose the Autumn Nourish Bowl, which contained chickpeas, quinoa, and roasted brussels sprouts, and Tom selected the Harvest Bowl, with butternut squash, spinach, and wild rice. He went up to order, returning a few minutes later with their food and two brightly colored smoothies.

"Carrot or beetroot?" he asked, as he placed the food and drinks on the table.

"I'll take beet," Lacey said, smiling at Tom's British terminology.

He passed the bright red drink across the table to her, and Lacey tucked in to her meal.

"Mm, tahini," she said, as the bitter, creamy flavor danced across her tongue.

Tom seemed to be enjoying his food as well. His green eyes were fixed on the bowl, his honey-colored hair flopping over his face. It was getting too long, Lacey noted. It needed a trim.

"How did you know about this place?" Lacey asked as she swallowed a delicious mouthful of herby, lemony quinoa. "I'd never have thought to go up that random wooden staircase!"

"It's been here for years," Tom told her.

"You've visited Brighton a lot?"

"Norah went to uni here. Dad occasionally brought me on day trips to visit her. Especially in the summer."

"Oh," Lacey said.

The comment knocked her off guard. It wasn't exactly a big thing, but Tom had failed to mention he had any personal connection to Brighton at any point during their trip so far. And it wasn't that he was being deliberately evasive. He just never seemed compelled to spontaneously share certain things with her. Unless prompted, Tom would probably never tell her a thing about his past.

Lacey tried not to let it bother her.

After their food, they went for a long walk along the pebbly beach. Chester dashed about, weaving through the groups of people and wading into the ocean. The waves were much rougher in Brighton than in Wilfordshire, and he kept barking at them, as if frustrated by their unpredictability.

Tom and Lacey walked hand in hand between Brighton's two piers, their backs to the one that was full of fairground rides and casinos, approaching the other, which was a burnt relic half falling into the sea.

"Tom, I really love it here," Lacey said.

"I can tell," Tom said. "You've been happy all day."

Lacey paused. That wasn't strictly true. Maybe on the outside she'd appeared calm and happy, but inside she'd been super concerned and stuck on her father.

She was in the same county as him. This was the closest proximity she'd had to him in decades, at least that she was aware of. She knew his address. If she wanted to, she could visit his home tomorrow and knock on his door.

And while Lacey knew it would be for the best if she did, she also knew herself too well. When it came to her long-lost father, she was a coward. She'd eke the whole sorry situation out agonizingly, just as she had with sending the letter in the first place.

She just wasn't ready. She didn't have the guts for it. She couldn't take it if he rejected her for a second time. If he'd replied to her letter, it would be different. But it had been weeks since she'd written to him, and each day that had passed felt like she was being rejected by him all over again. It was too much. She just couldn't do it.

"We should probably think about finding an inn," Lacey said, her enthusiasm for the beach suddenly gone.

"Anything you want, my dear," Tom said, failing to pick up on her growing unease.

They wandered back up to the road until they found an inn with a sign in the window saying it was dog friendly. It was painted in the same pale green color as all the lamp posts and railings, and a rainbow flag waved over the door.

They went inside. The whole place was decorated like a shrine to cats. A fluffy white cat lay on the desk sleeping.

"Good evening!" exclaimed a flamboyant older gentleman at the reception desk. His white hair was coiffed up into a rockabilly doo, and he was wearing a patterned cravat.

His friendly eccentricity put Lacey immediately at ease.

"We'd like a room for two," she said.

Chester walked up to the counter and sniffed the sleeping cat. It opened a single eye before contentedly falling back to sleep.

"A room for two humans and one dog," the man said as he typed into a computer. "Yes, we can fit you all in. Will you be staying for breakfast? We do continental and fried."

"Fried," Lacey and Tom said at the same time.

They laughed.

The man handed them their room key and a little booklet. "The desk is manned all night. If you get peckish for a cheese toasty or glass of mojito your every wish can be fulfilled."

"Thank you so much," Lacey said, absolutely delighted by the man's showmanship. "How do we do that?"

"Just press one on your telephone and ask for David," he said.

At the sound of his name, Lacey immediately faltered. She'd forgotten all about telling her ex-husband about her upcoming nuptials. But now her mom knew, it wouldn't be long before he found out too.

He would have to wait. For now, Lacey wanted to hold onto her happiness and enjoy her time in the vibrant city of Brighton.

Because after this, Lacey thought with a shiver, they were just going to be closer and closer to confronting her dad after all these years.

CHAPTER SEVEN

"I'm stuffed," Lacey announced, putting her knife and fork neatly on her empty breakfast plate.

Tom and Lacey had just shared a wonderful full English fried breakfast at their inn, consisting of eggs, toast, beans, tomatoes, sausages, mushrooms, and hash browns. Though Lacey hadn't said it aloud, it was almost as good as Tom's fried breakfasts. Almost...

"Where shall we go today?" Tom asked.

Lacey secretly wanted to stay in Brighton, but she'd agreed to explore Sussex.

"I'd love to check out Hastings," she said. "People online seem to really like it."

Tom drained the last of his coffee. "Hastings it is. Are you ready to go?"

Lacey nodded.

Their bags were already packed, so all that was left to check out and pay. The flamboyant David bid them adieu, and they left the inn with Chester trotting along with them.

It must've rained all night, because the streets were soggy and dew drops clung to the foliage. They got back into the van and hit the road again, careful to avoid the large puddles caused by the overworked storm drains.

After a while, Tom turned them away from the ocean.

"I thought we were going to Hastings," Lacey said.

"I have a better idea," Tom replied.

Lacey folded her arms. "Which is...?"

"The Sussex Downs. It's a national park. A place of outstanding natural beauty, with a four-hundred-year-old woodland. The sort of place your romance authors spent all summer frolicking around."

Lacey chuckled. "But you know we can't paddleboard in the countryside," she teased.

Tom drove them along narrow roads up into the green undulating hills and valleys. Thanks to last night's downpour, the vegetation looked extremely lush, and as they went deeper and deeper into the hillsides, Lacey marveled at the woodlands filled with ancient-looking chestnut, ash, beech, and oak trees.

"It's beautiful," she gushed, as she gazed down the valley at the fields filled with sheep and cows.

Tom was right. Jane Austen would've frolicked to her heart's content in these hills. It was utterly charming.

"Shall we find a walking route?" Lacey asked Tom. "I'm sure Chester would love to stretch his legs."

Her canine companion was sitting straight-backed in the back seat of the van, gazing intently at the countryside. As an English Shepherd, this was the exact environment he was bred to be in. They were essentially in his ancestral home. It would run deep in his DNA.

"I'm pretty sure the sheep farmers would have something to say if we let Chester loose in their fields," Tom said. "And I know the interior of my van would prefer not to be covered in mud. Or pick up the smell of soggy dog."

"Good point." Lacey checked her rambler's app again. "Looks like there's a town just down the hill with a country pub. Want to go there instead?"

She knew how much her foodie fiancé loved to sample ale in the local pub.

"Sounds great," he said.

He drove the van down the hill into the town.

It was a gorgeous little place, with medieval architecture, crooked half-timber houses, and steep cobbled lanes. In fact, the quaint town was very reminiscent of Wilfordshire if you swapped the ocean for the hills, and turned the clock back in time a few hundred years. There were even ancient ruins of old stone buildings falling down and overtaken by grass.

"Wow, this place is gorgeous," Lacey said. "What's it called?"

But no sooner had she said it than a road sign on the grass verge appeared. Against a brown backdrop, in white writing, were the words: *Welcome to Rye.*

Instantly, Lacey's breath caught in her lungs.

"Rye?" she gasped.

This was where her father lived!

She looked over at Tom, stunned. "How did…"

Then she noticed the knowing look in Tom's eyes. This was no accident. He'd driven her here on purpose. He'd engineered the whole thing to get her here.

36

"Surprise," he said, cautiously.

Lacey's heart was racing so hard she felt like it would burst out of her chest. She didn't know what to say, what to think. Tom meant well, of course, but this was a shock to the system, as if he'd pushed her off a diving board into cold water.

"I know you said you weren't sure about coming here," Tom said, carefully. "But I also know how much having your dad at our wedding would mean to you."

He tapped down the indicator and turned onto a road. *Mermaid Street.*

Lacey squealed. Tom wasn't just taking her into Rye, he was driving her to her father's house!

"Tom?" she queried, her panic magnifying. "How did you…"

"How did I get the address?" he guessed. "You left your writing pad by the phone with the address on it."

She felt blindsided. She could hardly see straight.

Tom slowed the van to a halt in front of a cottage. He looked across at her. "Lacey, this is your dad's house."

*

Lacey peered through the passenger window at the small cottage. It was understated, reminiscent of Crag Cottage. Were all the answers to the questions she'd spent her life seeking inside?

"Lacey?" came Tom's gentle voice. "What do you want to do?"

Lacey hesitated. She felt like jelly. She wasn't even sure she'd be able to walk up to the door and knock, let alone face what happened when it was answered.

Just then, Chester wedged his way through the gap in the seats and sat in her lap. He nuzzled her with his nose, whining softly. Lacey knew what he was trying to tell her. It was now or never.

"I'm going to knock," Lacey said decisively, announcing her intentions.

She opened the van door and hopped down, surprised to find her legs sturdy beneath her. A sense of resolve came from nowhere.

Lacey paced slowly up the garden path, taking in every detail with pin-point precision. From the ankle-high shrubs and ferns dotting the unkempt grass, to the wooden lean-to style porch arch surrounding the front door. Inside the lean-to, there was a pair of muddy men's hiking boots on the welcome mat, and a faded sculpture of a garden gnome

37

holding a fishing rod. Lacey was able to see every little detail in sharp technicolor. All the little signs of a life being lived. It felt like the gaps in her mind about her father were being filled in.

The front door was wooden, painted in glossy blue paint that was flecking in places. A wonky rusty silver letter flap. A door-knocker in a similar state of rust. The cottage was rustic to say the least.

Lacey took a deep breath. Then she knocked.

At first everything was silent. Then Lacey heard a shuffling noise coming from inside. Someone was there.

Her mouth went dry with apprehension.

With a click, scrape, and creak, the door opened up. Standing before Lacey was a man.

He was bald. Wrinkled.

And he was not her father.

All the air went out of Lacey's lungs in one sudden whoosh. Her hands started to shake. It wasn't him. It wasn't her dad.

The man was about a foot too short, a decade too old, and had the wrong color eyes.

"Can I help you, young lady?" he asked in a strong British accent.

Lacey staggered. The surprise had knocked her for six.

"I'm sorry, I think I've got the wrong address," she mumbled. "I thought someone different lived here."

She turned to leave.

"You must be looking for Frank," the man said.

Lacey froze. Her heart started beating against her sternum like a jackhammer.

She turned and looked back at the stranger.

"That's right," she said, trying to play it off casually. "Do you know him?"

"He was the previous tenant," the man said.

Previous tenant? Lacey echoed in her mind. Her father had moved. She'd missed him.

"Do you know where he moved?" she asked, feeling suddenly desperate.

"No, sorry, I don't. Are you a friend of his?"

Lacey couldn't speak. After all the leads she'd followed, all the painstaking puzzle pieces she'd put together, to discover her father was no longer there was a bombshell she couldn't process. All she could manage was a zombie-like nod.

The man smiled. "Well, you just missed him. He left a couple of weeks back."

That was the final straw for Lacey's fragile mind. She was just weeks too late? If she hadn't dragged her feet at every single step of the way, she wouldn't have been too late.

Lacey's legs turned weak. Her head began to swim. Suddenly, it felt like there wasn't enough oxygen in the air. Lacey felt faint and grabbed the wall to steady herself.

"Oh dear," the man said, sounding concerned. "Are you okay? You've gone pale. Can I get you a glass of water?"

Lacey couldn't answer him. She was hyperventilating.

Suddenly, Tom was there. He must've spotted her looking faint from the van.

She felt his hand on her back. Then Chester started nuzzling her with his nose, providing reassuring comfort.

"Lacey?" Tom said, softly. "What happened?"

Lacey grabbed him with a trembling hand.

"It's not him," she said, gasping for oxygen. "He's gone. Moved. My dad's gone."

She'd come so close to finding her father, but because of her cowardice, she'd missed her chance.

She gazed into Tom's eyes, seeing her own pain mirrored in his empathy.

The man on the doorstep spoke softly. "Frank is your father?"

"Yes…" Lacey told him, breathlessly. "I haven't seen him for decades. I traced him to this address."

The man let out a gasp of sympathy. "I'm so sorry."

He spoke with such genuine compassion, Lacey felt it right in the deepest part of her heart. Her panic began to subside.

"Maybe you should come in?" the man added. "Both of you. I've barely decorated so it's more or less the way your father left it. Do you want to see what the cottage looked like when he lived here?"

It was a kind offer. Lacey was genuinely touched. Perhaps there'd be some clue Frank had left behind for her. Maybe there was a chance her trail hadn't gone completely cold.

"Come on," the man said, invitingly. "I'll stick the kettle on and make us a brew."

He turned and headed inside, leaving the door gaping open.

Tom's squeezed Lacey's shoulder. She knew he was trying to comfort her but she couldn't help feeling annoyed with him. She'd made it perfectly clear she didn't want to come here, and he hadn't listened to her. He'd pushed her into it. No, it wasn't his fault her dad had moved on, but it was his fault that he'd pushed her to take one step more than she was comfortable with taking.

Without looking at him, Lacey stepped inside the cottage, and Tom's hand fell from her shoulder.

CHAPTER EIGHT

Lacey could hardly hide her disappointment as the man who was not her father entered the living room with three mugs of tea clutched in his hands. He placed them down on a wooden coffee table covered in cup ring stains. Liquid spilled down the sides of the mugs, adding yet more marks.

"That's proper Yorkshire tea," the man announced. "I don't drink that awful pre-bagged stuff. Blergh."

He smiled, and Lacey forced herself to smile, too, though inside she felt despondent. On the sofa beside her, Tom seemed too straight-backed and formal, like he could sense the unhappiness radiating off of her and felt responsible for it. And as loath as Lacey was to admit it, she did kind of hold him responsible. She'd said all along she didn't want to come here, in case of this very situation. Tom had gone against her wishes by bringing her here, and it left a bad taste in her mouth.

On the sofa opposite Lacey and Tom, a tabby cat leapt up onto the man's knees and began bumping its head against his hand, demanding to be petted.

"This darn stray," he said, affectionately rubbing the cat behind the ears. "Came with the house. I expect your father was feeding her, because she wanders into my kitchen at six a.m. and meows the house down until I give her breakfast."

Lacey tried to visualize the scene, but came up blank. Yes, her father had been an early riser, but a cat lover? She had no memory of that at all. Maybe it had never come up because they lived in a New York City apartment. Or maybe he'd grown to love them since moving to the UK. Either way, the insignificant detail felt suddenly like a huge gaping hole in her knowledge, and only further sent Lacey into a tailspin.

At the risk of a full-blown emotional breakdown, Lacey took one of the mugs from the table and sipped slowly, using it to cover her face. An uncomfortable silence descended, filled only with the sound of Lacey's slurping.

Tom shifted on the couch. "May I ask you a question?"

He was in Genial-English-Gentleman-Mode, Lacey noted. He always did this when he was uncomfortable.

"Fire away," the man said, as he continued petting the overly affectionate stray cat.

"Have you been getting Frank's mail?" Tom asked.

Lacey glared at him. She understood what he was getting at, that perhaps the letter she'd mailed here for her father had arrived too late for him, but for some reason it felt far too personal to be spoken of aloud. It felt to Lacey like she had a gaping wound and Tom had just ripped off the bandage, exposing it to the elements.

"Bits and bobs," the man replied. "I asked the landlady for a forwarding address, but she says that Frank left her next to no personal information."

"No forwarding address?" Tom asked.

His question felt like a knife twisting in Lacey's guts.

The man shook his head. "Nothing. He was here one minute. Then the next, he disappeared."

Lacey could take it no more. She stood, abandoning the tea on the coffee table.

Here one minute, disappeared the next. Just like when she was a kid.

"I'm sorry," she mumbled, "I have to go. Th—thanks for the tea."

Tears blurred her vision as she rushed out of the living room and bolted for the front door. She heard the murmuring of Tom's voice in the background, presumably apologizing for their intrusion, but she could hardly hear it, because her pulse was pounding in her ears, drowning everything else out.

She pulled open the latch of the cottage door and hurried along the path, right around the back of the van where she was out of sight. She bent forward, her hands on her knees, and took huge gulps of air. She was either hyperventilating or on the cusp of a panic attack.

Just then, Tom appeared. "Lacey," he said, his face etched with worry. "I'm so sorry. I shouldn't have forced this on you."

Lacey peered up at him, hot tears stinging her eyes.

"I want to go home," she said. "Please. Let's just go home."

*

42

Lacey sat slumped in the passenger seat, gazing out at the dappled trees as they drove. Out the corner of her eye, she saw Tom give her yet another anxious glance.

"I'm so sorry about what happened back in Rye," he said for the umpteenth time since they'd set off for home.

"It's not your fault," Lacey said. She petted Chester's ears. He was sitting in the footwell, staying close to her as if intuitively sensing she needed his comfort. "I shouldn't have dragged my heels."

She just couldn't forgive herself for having missed him by a matter of weeks. Now, without a forwarding address, she might never find him.

She swallowed the hard lump that had formed in her throat.

The drive had been quiet, the atmosphere somber. Barely any words had passed between her and Tom, and Lacey hated how tense and uncomfortable it felt. She was relieved when she saw the sign for Exeter and knew they'd be home within the hour.

Suddenly, Tom slammed on the brakes. Lacey jerked forward, her seat belt locking. She instinctively threw her arm out to keep Chester from flying through the windshield. As the van halted, she was flung back against the seatback.

"Oof," she said, rubbing her chest, looking at her dog to make sure he was okay. "What was that for?"

"The road is flooded," Tom said. "Look."

Sure enough, the downwardly inclined road was submerged with water. Last night's downpour had evidently covered a wide area.

"Great," Lacey said. She desperately wanted to get home and put the terrible day behind her. "Now what?"

"I guess we'll have to find a different route," Tom said.

Sighing, Lacey checked the map app on her phone for a new route. She found one a little off the beaten path that took them around the outskirts of Exeter. Annoyingly for Lacey, it would add an extra thirty minutes to their long, awkward journey.

Lacey relayed the directions to Tom and he reversed the van to a small passing point before making a three-point turn (or ten-point turn, Lacey counted) and setting off on the new route.

They hadn't gotten far when they passed a row of shops, which were more like sheds, their structure made of part brick, part wood. Lacey realized they were converted barns, and each store had a little sign above the door. One, a hand-painted sign of chunky black writing on a beech wood backdrop, read: *Chumley's Antiques.*

"Hey, look at that," Tom said, noticing it too. "There's an antiques store. Wanna go in?"

Normally, this was the sort of thing Lacey would jump at. A cute little store tucked away off the beaten path? It was ripe for finding treasure! But she was still reeling from earlier.

She shook her head. "I'm not in the mood."

"Come on," Tom cajoled. "It will cheer you up! You know it will."

There was no arguing with that. Antique hunting was a guaranteed way for Lacey to forget about her troubles, even if for only a few minutes.

Without waiting for an answer, Tom pulled into the parking lot—which was really just a patch of dirt with white lines painted on it—parking beside a dark red Jeep Cherokee. The Jeep had only just arrived; its red brake lights were lit and its engine was belching fumes. By the look of the splattered mud all over its body and wheels, it had had no issue traversing the flooded road to get here.

"You don't see many of those in England," Tom said, peering at the Jeep as he killed the engine.

Lacey opened her door at the exact moment that the Jeep driver opened his. They almost clipped one another, but Lacey managed to pull hers back in the nick of time.

"Hey!" the Jeep driver snapped, glaring at her. "Watch it!"

Lacey raised her eyebrows as the angry man slammed his door shut and marched inside Chumley's antiques store.

"How rude," Tom said.

"I guess someone's having a worse day than me," Lacey commented, wryly.

They exited the van with Chester and headed inside Chumley's.

Inside, the shop had wooden floorboards covered in patterned, dusty rugs. A big fat ginger cat slept in a Victorian-era fabric chair. It raised its head apathetically at the new customers and their dog, before going back to sleep.

Lacey noticed the Jeep driver was at the counter, waiting for assistance, impatiently drumming his fingers on the counter. She went the opposite direction in order to keep her distance, and began perusing the shelves.

"Scalextrics!" Tom exclaimed, looking at a replica racing track with little cars on it. "Did you ever play with this?"

Lacey shook her head as he picked up a chunky plastic controller and pushed on the levers. With a loud electric crackle the cars started shooting around the track. Chester barked and wagged his tail excitedly as each car completed a lap and whizzed past him.

"I used to collect these things obsessively," Tom said. "I'd make the racetracks go all the way around the house. It drove Norah mad whenever she visited."

Bringing up Norah now, when Lacey was already feeling alienated from Tom, felt like just another wedge between them.

Tom was so distracted, he didn't even notice when Lacey turned and continued on, gazing at the shelves of the store.

Most of its stock was bric-a-brac, the sort of stuff that wouldn't fetch much more than a buck or two. She did see a couple of unique tchotchkes here and there but nothing worth parting with any money.

She was about to give up and ask Tom if they could leave when she spotted an oil painting depicting a bowl of tomatoes.

Immediately, Lacey was reminded of her father's special roasted tomato soup. For the first time since her awful discovery in Rye, Lacey felt her lips twitch up into a smile.

She paced over and picked up the wooden frame, holding the painting out in front of her. Just looking at it lifted her spirits. And It only cost a few bucks.

Lacey made a decision. She would buy the painting and hang it in the store, as a reminder of her father.

She headed over to the counter. The proprietor—an older man with two tufts of white hair sprouting out either side of his head—was still dealing with the rude Jeep driver. It seemed as if the customer was attempting to sell him something, and was using a pretty aggressive haggling style to do it.

"I'm sorry," the elderly man was saying, shaking his head, "but I don't buy jewelry. I don't know enough about it."

He seemed flustered, Lacey noted, like this had been going on for quite some time.

"This is a twenty-four-karat-gold engagement ring," the Jeep man replied gruffly. "You don't need to be an expert to know twenty-four-karat gold is valuable!"

The poor old man looked intimidated.

"I'm just not interested," he said.

At last, the Jeep driver realized he wasn't getting anywhere. He scoffed loudly then turned to leave.

In his haste, he barged right into Lacey.

Rather than apologize, he barked, "Watch it!" His gaze fell to the painting in Lacey's hand and he scoffed. "No surprises there. You have terrible taste."

He elbowed his way past her.

"Hey!" Tom snapped. "How dare you speak to her like that?"

The man glowered at Tom. Lacey could see the muscles of his biceps bulging in the sleeves of his T-shirt.

"Leave it," she murmured to Tom, touching his chest lightly to prompt him to stay back.

The man sneered. "I'd listen to the little lady if I were you."

And with that, he marched out of the shop muttering angrily under his breath.

"Jerk," Tom commented.

Lacey could feel the anger radiating off Tom. Perhaps on a better day she might've appreciated his protective fiancé routine, but considering everything that had happened in Rye, she wasn't particularly impressed.

Besides, with the day she was having, some random man being rude to her really had negligible impact on her mood.

"Hey, you found something," Tom commented, pointing at the tomato painting as if trying to change the subject.

"It's for the store," Lacey told him.

"It's cute," Tom said.

"I guess." She didn't feel like explaining the real reason for the purchase—that it would be a reminder to Lacey of the father she'd failed to find, and would most likely never be able to track down.

Just then, Lacey noticed something tucked under Tom's arm.

"What are you getting?" she asked.

Tom's cheeks went pink. He held up a box. It was the Scalextric set. "I just couldn't refuse."

Of course, Lacey thought. Tom's Scalextric obsession she'd only just found out about. Maybe if she knew him better, she'd've immediately known he would buy it. It would be a joyful moment they could both share in. Instead, it was just another blow to Lacey. Another reminder that so much of Tom was a mystery to her.

CHAPTER NINE

It was dark by the time the cliffs of Wilfordshire appeared through the windshield. The sight of her craggy, cliffside town gave Lacey a jolt of comfort, one she desperately needed after the day she'd had.

"Can you drop me off at the shop?" she asked Tom. "I want to hang my painting. And double-check that Gina and Finn didn't burn the place to the ground."

"Sure," Tom said with an air of melancholy.

Lacey knew that he still felt bad about what happened earlier with her failed attempt to find her father. It wasn't his fault that Frank had moved on, but Lacey couldn't help but feel slightly aggrieved that he'd duped her into it in the first place. Added to all the stuff she'd learned about him in Brighton, she also felt a little alienated. Distant. She needed a bit of space.

Tom turned onto the cobblestoned high street. It was looking peculiarly bare now the summer bunting had been removed from the lampposts. The planters were also empty now that the summer wildflowers had died back.

"I guess I should check in at the patisserie, too," Tom said, as they bobbed along the uneven ground. "See how Emmanuel got along with the macron pumpkin for the display."

Normally, Lacey would make some funny quip about Tom's ever changing macaron window display, but she wasn't in the mood. The distance between them felt like a gaping chasm.

As the van bumped along the high street's cobblestones, Chester suddenly awakened. He drew himself to sitting, his ears pricked. Clearly he recognized the bumpy feel beneath the tires and knew it meant home. He let out an excited bark.

"That's right, boy," Lacey told him. "Let's go and see how well cousin Boudica did at babysitting the humans."

Tom parked. Lacey grabbed her new painting, gave Tom a quick peck on the cheek, then hopped out of the van, Chester slinking out after her.

47

"No smell of smoke," she told him, as they rounded the corner toward the store. "Oh, and no sign of flames, either. Perhaps we got away with it."

She pushed open the door and walked into the midst of a heated debate.

"I told you fifty times!" Gina was yelling at Finnbar, flapping her arms around.

"And *then* you told me that *you* were going to do it yourself!" Finnbar screeched back.

He was standing on a stepladder, his back to Lacey, fussing over one of the display shelves.

"I never said such a thing!" Gina cried.

"Guys!" Lacey shouted over the top of both of them. "What's going on?"

Silence fell in an instant. Finnbar froze, then slowly craned his head over his shoulder. Gina spun to face the door, seeming to shrink as she did so. Lacey knew that face all too well from her rambunctious nephew, Frankie. It was the look a kid gave their parents when they were caught with their hand in the forbidden cookie jar.

Lacey put her hands on her hips. "Tell me what happened. Right now."

Finnbar and Gina exchanged a nervous glance, then Finnbar trotted down his stepladder and revealed a giant hole in the wall.

Lacey's mouth dropped open.

"W—why is there a hole in my wall?" she stammered, in disbelief.

Her gaze fell to a pool of porcelain shards on the floor that told her more than one piece of antique crockery had been destroyed in the process of the aforementioned hole coming into existence, and it took all her strength not to curse.

Finnbar and Gina started speaking at the same time, so quickly Lacey couldn't understand a word either was saying. She couldn't tear her horrified gaze away from the gaping hole in the brickwork, the plaster it had sprayed all over the floor, and the broken merchandise.

With a wave of anger, Lacey held her hand up, palm forward, in the gesture of silence.

Her guilty employees immediately ceased their bickering.

Lacey looked first to Gina. In the calmest voice she could muster, she asked again, more slowly, "Why is there a hole in my wall?"

"Well, you know that air conditioning system Taryn wanted to put in," Gina began.

"Yes..." Lacey said between her teeth. "The one I told her to send me a quote for before she did anything. That one. What about it?"

"What? She said you'd given it the go-ahead, and arranged for her workmen to knock through a hole to mount the unit into," Gina blurted.

A rush of fury washed from Lacey's head to the tip of her toes. Of all of Taryn's dirty little tricks, this one really took the cake. Deceiving her. Lying to her employees. Going behind her back. Damaging her property. If Lacey hadn't already been in a state of emotional distress over everything that had happened earlier, she might've called Tom's lawyer mom, Heidi, for some advice on how to sue her evil neighbor for every penny she was worth.

But as it stood, having a hole knocked into her wall without her consent wasn't actually the worst thing that had happened to her that day. There were far more challenging things for Lacey to care about.

Lacey rubbed her forehead as she surveyed the mess of crockery smashed across the floor. "Did neither of you geniuses think to move the crockery that was in the way, at the very least?"

Immediately, the argument erupted between the two of them again.

"I asked Finn to do it," Gina said.

"But then she said she'd do it herself," Finnbar countered.

"But that was before I realized Boudica needed her walkies, and so I asked you to do it again."

"That's not right! I asked *you* if it wouldn't clash with Boudica's walkies and you said it wouldn't."

If there wasn't a gaping hole in Lacey's wall and a bunch of smashed pottery all over the floor, she may have found it amusing listening to two grown adults bicker over the timing of a dog's "walkies." But as it was, Lacey had neither the time nor the patience for their shenanigans.

"Could you fetch me a nail and hammer?" she said calmly to Finnbar.

He looked petrified. "You're not going to bash my head in with it, are you?" he asked in a meek voice.

"No," Lacey coolly. "But don't think for a minute that I don't want to."

Finnbar scurried away.

Lacey turned to Gina. "And you. Get the dustpan and brush. If you sweep the pieces carefully, we may be able to salvage something with hot glue."

She didn't even dare to look and see which pots were broken. That would have to wait for another day, when she was feeling less emotionally fraught.

Gina scampered away.

They both returned a moment later, nudging one another out of the way with their elbows in their haste to be the one who fixed the problem for their furious boss.

Lacey rolled her eyes at the pair of them.

While Gina began carefully sweeping up the broken pots, Lacey instructed Finnbar to hang the painting over the hole.

"Oh!" Gina exclaimed when she saw it. "Tomatoes."

Finnbar stepped back from the painting. At which point it suddenly slipped from the nail and crashed to the floor, snapping the wooden frame at one corner. Lacey sunk her face into her hand.

"I'm so sorry, I'm so sorry!" Finnbar cried, running to pick up the painting.

"Don't," Lacey said. How had she managed to hire such a klutz? Being clumsy was pretty much the last quality one would want in an employee of an antiques store.

He looked mortified. Lacey couldn't help but take pity on him. "It was only five bucks. Don't worry."

She went over to retrieve the painting before Finnbar could accidentally make the situation even worse than it already was. But as she picked the painting up, the weakened part of the frame gave way entirely, and the entire side snapped clean off.

That's when Lacey noticed the corner of the canvas was curling up. It appeared as if the painting had been framed on top of another one.

She took hold of the corner and pulled.

"Lacey!" Gina exclaimed. "I know we've disappointed you but destroying your painting is hardly the right way to go about it!"

"I'm not destroying it," Lacey countered. "Look, there's something underneath."

Her employees crowded either side of her shoulders, peering down as she continued carefully moved the painting of the tomatoes away.

When she was done, she gasped with astonishment.

The painting staring at them was a portrait of a woman, capturing the beauty of raw emotion in a way only a few of the greatest portrait artists could manage—the Lucian Freuds and Frida Kahlos of the world.

"Wow," she heard from either side of her.

At least her two warring employees were unified in the awesomeness of the find.

Lacey squinted at the signature. "Carson Desi?" she said. "I've never heard of him."

Finnbar let out a strange noise of shock. "I have."

Lacey turned to look at him. "Oh?"

Finnbar nodded slowly, his eyes wide like he'd seen a ghost. "Lacey, you're holding a priceless painting!"

CHAPTER TEN

"Here," Gina said, handing Lacey a chamomile tea.

They were sitting in the store, in a circle as if sitting around a campfire, with the Carson Desi painting in the middle of them.

"Tell me again," Lacey said to Finnbar, "what's the deal with this guy?"

"He's a British artist," Finnbar explained. "Hugely popular in the sixties and seventies. But by the eighties he'd vanished. And the funny thing was he was extremely private, and kept his identity hidden."

"Like Banksy?" Gina asked.

Lacey frowned at her older friend. "How do you know who Banksy is?"

"I keep up with culture," Gina replied, adjusting the red-framed spectacles she'd purchased from the hipster-haven of Shoreditch in London.

"He was a British artist?" Lacey asked, turning back to Finnbar. "But Desi isn't a British surname, is it?"

Finnbar shook his head. "It's Indonesian in origin."

"And no one had any inkling who he was?" Lacey asked.

"No one in the public. I assume there were agents and galleries behind the scenes who knew his identity, but to the rest of the world, he was a mystery. The mystique just helped drive up the price of his works."

Lacey looked at the gorgeous painting. The woman it depicted wasn't a traditional beauty by any means—her nose was crooked, her eyebrows were thick and unkempt, and she had a figure fuller than the ideal—but that only made the painting even better. The artist had perfectly captured the model's own personal, unique beauty, right down to the crinkles beside her eyes and mouth, that gave her a knowing look. It really was an exceptional piece of art, created by the hand of a genius.

"How do we know it's not a replica?" Lacey asked.

"Because that painting was never publicized," Finnbar explained, drawing on his fountain of knowledge. "You can't fake a painting without the original, can you?"

52

"Okay, then maybe someone just copied Desi's style to create something that looked like it could be his?"

Finnbar gave her a look. "Trust me, Lacey. That's an original."

Gina nudged her excitedly. "Lacey, you're going to make a windfall with that!"

As Gina and Finnbar excitedly discussed the painting, Lacey fell into a quiet, contemplative rumination, fretting over keeping the painting. On the one hand, the painting was hers fair and square. But on the other, could she really keep it when the old man she'd purchased it from had no idea it was there? If she returned it, she'd be walking away from a fortune. But if she didn't, it would be akin to stealing a fortune from right under the nose of an innocent man.

"Wait until the press hears about this," Finnbar said, loud enough to cut through Lacey's anxious thoughts.

"Press?" she asked.

"Um, yes!" Finnbar said, eyes wide. He'd become more animated since the discovery of the painting than Lacey had ever seen him.

"It will cause a storm in the art world," Finnbar continued. "'Woman breaks antique: finds priceless painting hidden beneath.' I can see the headlines already! You know, I know some people who work at Tate. Maybe I could call them."

Lacey shook her head. "No. No press. No Tate Gallery. I don't want anyone finding out about this."

Finnbar paused. "I don't understand. People are going to find out. A missing Desi isn't the sort of thing you'll be able to quietly brush under the carpet."

For a moment, Lacey let herself fantasize about all the things she could do with the money from the painting—which, if what Finnbar was telling her really was correct—would make her a millionaire. She'd be able to buy Tom's seaside house. A Regency manor house on the Brighton seafront. She could probably buy herself a home in every English coastal town, if she wanted to. She'd be able to put enough money in Frankie's college fund for him to attend an Ivy League. She could buy a whole new sanctuary for Alice, her adopted donkey, and all her donkey friends.

She would also become part of the lore of Carson Desi. An extra paragraph in the textbooks written on him forevermore. It was appealing, to say the least.

But something else was telling Lacey not to. Her father.

Along with his tomato soup, one of the most vivid memories she had of him was the time he'd told her that doing what was right was always more important than what was easy.

"I'm not keeping it," Lacey blurted.

Finnbar glanced over at Gina, looking utterly perplexed.

Gina shook her head. "Here we go again. This is the Roman coin all over again, isn't it?"

"I bought it off an old man," Lacey explained. "An old man whose antiques store was basically in a barn. He can't have known the Desi was hidden behind the tomato picture when he sold it to me. I have to return it."

"Are you crazy?" Finnbar exclaimed.

"She always does this," Gina told him. "Always takes the moral high road."

"You say it like it's a bad thing," Lacey interjected. "Having a clear conscience to me is worth more than all the money in the world. And it's not like I'm struggling here. The store's doing great. I don't need to steal from an old man to keep food on the table!"

Gina rolled her eyes. "So dramatic."

"You could auction it," Finnbar cut in. "That way you could give the proceeds to the man and still walk away with a healthy fee in commission."

"I could…" Lacey said, allowing herself to briefly deliberate. But then she shook her head and found her resolve. "No. It wouldn't be right. If he wants me to auction it, then that's something we can discuss when I return it to him. It's not my decision to make."

Gina shook her head. "Sorry, Finn, you'll learn this about Lacey. Once she's made up her mind about something, there's no talking her out of it. Even if it is in her best interests."

Finnbar's shoulders slumped. But Lacey wasn't about to back down just because her history buff employee wanted her to! She was going to do what was right. And that meant tomorrow, she'd drive back out to the barn on the outskirts of Exeter, and return the Desi to the old man.

She glanced at it again. The woman's expression seemed to be telling Lacey something different than she'd read in it before. It seemed to be a knowing look, a look of self-assuredness. It seemed to be thanking Lacey for making the right decision.

CHAPTER ELEVEN

Lacey's alarm clock sounded. She opened her eyes sleepily and heaved herself up.

She'd slept terribly last night, fretting constantly over the trip to Rye and how much of a failure it had ended up being.

She thought about calling Tom to catch him up on everything that had happened last night with the discovery of the painting, but she really didn't feel like talking to him right now. She knew it wasn't his fault that her father had moved on, but she still felt annoyed with him for forcing her hand when she wasn't ready.

Deciding she'd spent enough time stressing out, Lacey kicked the covers off.

She disturbed Chester, who let out a noise of displeasure.

"Sorry, boy," she said. "Come on, let's have breakfast, then we're going to drive out to the countryside."

They headed down to the kitchen to complete their morning routines—coffee for Lacey and kibble for Chester, followed by a shower for Lacey and pee in the garden for Chester—then climbed into the car and drove back to the countryside shack, the precious Desi painting in the passenger seat.

She paused, looking over at the woman with the crooked nose and knowing smile. Was she crazy for returning it? But no, she remembered her dad's words and knew she was doing the right thing.

When Lacey reached Chumley's and parked, the store looked even more dilapidated than she remembered. It wasn't quite as sunny today as it had been when she and Tom had first visited, and without the big Jeep Cherokee in the parking lot, she could see more of the damaged brickwork and the climbing ivy the converted barn was losing its battle against.

Lacey felt even more certain she was doing the right thing by returning the painting to the old man. He was clearly struggling financially.

She headed inside the store. The old man was sitting behind the counter going through his books. He looked up at her, and a look of recognition flashed in his eyes.

"Back again?" he asked. "I suppose you want a refund?"

He said it without malice. Lacey shook her head. How stingy would she have to be to drive all this way just to get her five bucks back?

"Not at all!" she exclaimed.

The man's expression turned to curiosity. "Oh? Then how can I help you?"

"I came to show you this," Lacey said.

She laid the painting gently across his counter.

The man stood and moved his spectacles from his head to the bridge of his nose. As he peered at the painting, his eyes widened. He gasped.

"Is that…"

"…a Carson Desi," Lacey finished. "Yes. It is."

"If you want to sell it to me," the man said, "then I'm afraid I don't have the money to afford it. Best to take that to one of the big auction houses."

Lacey chuckled and shook her head.

"I'm not trying to sell it," she said, recalling the aggressive engagement ring seller who'd been in here the last time she'd visited. "It's yours. I came to return it to you."

The old man looked thoroughly perplexed. "I think you're mistaken, my dear."

In response, Lacey held up the broken frame the tomato painting had been in. "I found it hidden behind the painting I bought yesterday."

A whole range of emotions passed across the man's face in such quick succession it was hard to keep up with. He went from confusion, to surprise, to acceptance, to… distaste?

"It's yours," he said, flippantly, waving a dismissive hand. "You paid for it. You keep it."

Lacey was surprised. This wasn't the reaction she'd been expecting. She'd thought the man would be thrilled to have an expensive painting returned to him!

"I don't think you understand," she said. "This is worth a lot of money."

"I understand," he said, just as dismissively as before.

Lacey frowned. As far as she could tell, he didn't understand at all. This was a priceless painting!

"I don't mean a fancy spa day's worth of money," Lacey explained. "I mean a lot. Like a lot a lot."

"I understand," the man said again, with emphasis. A smile twitched on his lips. "But I don't want it."

Lacey just couldn't comprehend what he was telling her. He knew the painting was worth a lot of money but he didn't want it back?

"But w—why?" she stammered.

The man smiled mournfully. "I'm old. I'm on my last legs. There's no use for money up there." He pointed a wizened finger up to the heavens.

"But what about your family?" Lacey challenged. "You could treat them to holidays. Houses. Help your grandkids get on the property ladder."

"I don't have any grandkids," he replied. "And I don't have any kids for that matter, either. My dear wife passed away seven years ago, after thirty wonderful years of marriage. It's just me."

"I'm so sorry," Lacey, feeling saddened by his story. "But there must be something you need. What about your cat?" She gestured to the fluffy ginger beast sleeping on a shelf behind him.

"Tibbles is spoiled enough as it is. Trust me. I'm happy with my lot. I don't need the hassle that comes with money. I've watched a lot of decent folks lose themselves to greed, and I've seen a lot of relationships deteriorate because of it. I'm happier without it. Trust me."

Finally, it sunk in what he was telling her. But Lacey simply didn't feel right walking away with a painting worth enough to change this entire man's life.

"Then we're at an impasse," she said. "Because I can't take it. Especially now I've heard your story. So I have a suggestion, if you'll hear me out."

"Oh?" the man said.

"I suggest you re-hide the painting behind another, just like how I found it. Then you can put it up on your wall as a little secret. It would make you smile every time you looked at it."

At this, the old man began to chuckle.

"You're a curious young woman," he said. "And I can see you're not backing down. Then yes. Okay. I will do that. It can be our secret." He tapped his nose.

Then, to Lacey's surprise, the elderly man gave her a hug.

Feeling glad she'd done the right thing, she left him her business card in case he wanted to stay in touch.

Lacey smiled the whole drive back to Wilfordshire, glad she'd been a Good Samaritan and hadn't let Finnbar or Gina talk her into keeping the painting, or selling it and donating the money to the old man. The human connection had meant far more to her than the money ever would.

But as she turned onto the high street and drove down the cobbled streets to her store, she was surprised to see a crowd of people spilling from the sidewalk into the road, and taking up her usual parking spot.

She took the side road, craning her head as she passed to see what was going on. Was one of them holding a boom? And another a video camera? What on earth...?

Confused and slightly anxious, Lacey parked and killed the engine.

"Come, come," she said to Chester, as she hopped out of the car.

He hurried after her, keeping close to her heels as they rounded the corner. He'd gone into guard dog mode, something he always did whenever she gave off vibes of suspicion.

As Lacey drew closer to the store, there was no doubt at all what was happening. A person was holding a large fluffy boom mic on a stand, another holding a large black camera, and they were both standing beside a white van with the logo of the local Wilfordshire news station painted on it. The female reporter Lacey recognized from their light-hearted fluff pieces was standing right in front of her store.

"Just last night, a genuine Carson Desi was discovered in this very store!" the news reporter exclaimed. "It came as a complete surprise to the store's owner, who discovered the painting hidden beneath another. The painting of a woman by the famously reclusive artist is rumored not to have been part of his known collection. Once valued by a professional, the painting may well go down in the history books as one of England's largest sales."

Fury rolled in Lacey's stomach. She'd expressly said "no press." But one of her employees had blabbed anyway. She was going to find out which one.

CHAPTER TWELVE

Lacey was furious that one of her employees had gone behind her back and contacted the press. Not wanting to be seen by the news crew, Lacey beelined for the back gate to her store. But she hadn't made it ten paces when the news reporter caught sight of her.

"And here's the lucky proprietor herself!" the woman exclaimed.

A swarm of people and equipment came at Lacey. As a microphone was shoved under her nose, Lacey took a step back, feeling suddenly overwhelmed.

"Annabella Josher," the reporter announced, grinning a big smile with huge white veneered teeth that glinted in the sunlight. "*Wilfordshire Weekly* on Your TV. Tell us about your incredible find."

Despite her friendly expression, her tone was actually demanding. The mismatch was rather disconcerting. Even Chester picked up on it. He began to emit a low growl.

"There's nothing to tell," Lacey told the woman sternly. "You've been misinformed."

Annabella laughed uncomfortably. She patted her blonde bouffant. This clearly wasn't going how she was expecting. Most people jumped at the chance to be on TV. Most people weren't guarded, like Lacey.

"Someone's playing coy," Annabella Josher said to the camera, letting out a slightly hysterical giggle.

Lacey cringed at the thought of her face being beamed into the living rooms of the locals.

"I'm not playing it coy," she said, firmly. "The painting has been returned to its rightful owner. I no longer have it."

Annabella's perfectly shaped eyebrows rose up her perfectly smooth forehead. "Did I just hear you correctly? You gave away a famous Carson Desi painting? To whom?"

Lacey flashed narrowed eyes. "None of your business."

And with that, she marched away, leaving the news reporter floundering on the sidewalk.

She just had time to overhear Annabella Josher exclaiming with fake enthusiasm, "You heard it here, folks. In a dramatic and unexpected development, it seems the Carson Desi painting has been reallocated once again!" before angrily shoving open the door.

The bell jangled above her as the door slammed shut behind her. She locked it to make sure the reporter didn't follow her.

"Finnbar!" Lacey bellowed. "Gina! Get out here!"

Finnbar tiptoed through the archway, his hands in the air like he was a thief caught mid-burglary. Gina, in contrast, marched out to the shop floor in her bright Wellington boots and patterned skirt, with her chin held high.

"You've met our entourage, I take it," Gina said.

"Which one of you did this!" Lacey yelled, gesturing to the window.

Outside, the news report was ongoing. Lacey's revelation about returning the painting had only given them more to talk about. Now they weren't just dealing with a priceless painting unearthed from secrecy, but they were also dealing with a surly shop owner who'd given the darn thing away. Lacey had accidentally poured fuel on the flame of this story. It would've been better if she'd said nothing at all.

"It wasn't me," Finnbar said. "I'm as surprised as you are to see them here!"

Lacey frowned, then looked at Gina.

"Don't look at me!" her friend refuted. "I didn't do it."

Lacey glowered from one to the next. Both looked innocent enough, but one of them had gone against her wishes, and they were only making it worse by not coming clean.

"You are on very thin ice," she said. "Both of you."

*

That night, Lacey slept fitfully. In her dream, she was standing in a swanky art gallery. The woman in the painting had come to life, and she was dancing in the middle of the hall. Suddenly the hall turned into a turn of the century ballroom, and the old store man was twirling the woman around like a ballerina.

Lacey watched as another man approached and tapped his shoulder, taking the next dance. The store owner gracefully handed the portrait woman over to the new gentleman, and as the music started and the pair spun, Lacey realized the new man was her father.

He looked just as she remembered him—tall, with thick dark hair and a twinkle of confidence in his eye.

60

Suddenly, the dancing pair spun too briskly and knocked into a vase on a plinth. It fell and smashed across the floor with an almighty smash.

Lacey startled awake to find Chester pawing at her. Her heart was racing. She must've been moaning in her sleep.

Just then, she heard a banging coming from downstairs. Chester began barking, running back and forth from the bed to her closed bedroom door.

Lacey hastily pulled back the covers and grabbed her bathrobe off the hook on the back of the door, realizing as she did that it was morning, albeit very early.

As she stepped out onto the landing, she heard the banging again, and finally realized it was knocking. Someone was at the door. Who would be calling this early?

She hurried down, Chester following along with her, and pulled the door open to a bright, chilly autumn morning.

Standing on her doorstep was Superintendent Turner.

"Karl," she said, surprised. "What are you doing here?"

"Do you know a gentleman by the name of Edwin Cross?"

Lacey shook her head. "No. Who is that?"

"He owns a store. Chumley's. Just outside of Exeter."

"Chumley's?" Lacey asked, surprised to hear the name of the antiques store she'd visited just a day earlier. "Yes, I know it. Is Edwin the owner? If he is, then yes I've met him on two occasions." She crossed her arms against the chilly air. "What is this about?"

"I'm afraid I have bad news," Superintendent Karl Turner said. "Edwin Cross has been discovered dead."

CHAPTER THIRTEEN

Lacey was stunned. She couldn't believe what she was hearing. How could Edwin be dead? He'd seemed as fit and healthy as an elderly man could when she'd seen him just yesterday.

Her head began to spin. Chester nudged his nose into her palm and gave it a reassuring lick. She petted his ears before bringing her focus back to Superintendent Turner standing on her doorstep.

"What happened?" she asked.

"The bin collectors found him this morning. Saw the poor guy lying on his shop floor through the window and called an ambulance."

Lacey's throat tightened with grief as an image of Edwin Cross lying sprawled on the floor of his antiques store appeared in her mind's eye.

"H—how did he die?" she stammered.

"The paramedics were expecting a slip and fall," Superintendent Turner said. "But once they'd broken their way in and checked him over, it became apparent he'd sustained a sharp blow to the head."

Lacey winced. She'd been expecting as much—the police wouldn't be on her doorstep if he'd simply passed away from old age, after all—but it was still a shock. She felt cold all over, as the blood drained from her face.

"He was murdered," she stated.

"It appears so."

A wave of nausea overcame Lacey. Who would want to harm such a sweet man? She couldn't think of anyone who less deserved to meet a violent end than Edwin Cross.

But somehow in the midst of her grief, a thought came to Lacey in a moment of sharp clarity. The police weren't just here to break the news of Edwin's demise to her. Something else had brought them to her doorstep on this chilly autumn morning. And Lacey had a suspicion she knew what it might be...

"Why are you here?" she asked. "Isn't this a matter for the Exeter cops?"

A faint smirk appeared on the detective's lips.

"I'm glad you asked," he said, looking distinctly like he was about to relish this moment. "You see, your business card was found in the victim's pocket. When the Exeter cops typed you into the system... bingo! Your fingerprints came up, and now we're involved as well."

Lacey cringed at his cavalier attitude. She knew her fingerprints were in the system from being erroneously charged in the past, but she'd never been convicted of anything, and she was no criminal. It seemed grossly unfair for her to be tarnished in that way.

"He had my business card because I gave it to him when I returned the painting," she explained.

"Ah, the painting," Karl Turner said. He'd clearly been waiting for her to bring it up. "A priceless Carson Desi, is that correct?"

"That's right," Lacey confirmed.

"Yes, I caught that segment on the local news," Superintendent Turner said. "I don't make a habit of watching Annabella Josher's light-hearted pieces, but that one was particularly interesting. Snapping at the reporter. Shouting at your employees. It seemed to me that you were rather ... agitated?"

Lacey cringed. Even she had to admit her behavior looked incriminating. Without the context of her feeling betrayed by one of her employees calling the press, her gruffness toward Annabella Josher, and subsequent outburst at Finnbar and Gina, would make her look suspicious in anyone's eyes.

"I was taken off guard," Lacey said, feeling her defenses starting to go up.

"Evidently," Superintendent Turner replied. "You might want to work on your on-screen presence."

"Thanks for the advice," Lacey replied, dryly. "Are we done here?"

"Far from it," Superintendent Turner replied, haughtily. "We're just getting started."

Lacey ground her teeth with irritation. Superintendent Turner was obviously hiding an ace card up his sleeve. He always did this; drip-fed her bits of information, riled her up like some kind of wind-up toy, then dropped a bomb and watched as she unraveled. To be playing his tricks now, when she was already grieving a man's death, seemed especially distasteful.

"What I'm wondering," Superintendent Turner continued, "is why you decided to return a priceless painting in the first place?"

"I can see why it might seem strange to someone like you," Lacey replied, "but there are actually some human beings on this earth who are fair and decent and know the difference between right and wrong."

Karl Turner barked out a nasty laugh.

"Here's the interesting thing," he said. "The painting isn't there."

Lacey's stomach plummeted to her toes. Her features fall.

"W—what?" she said.

"The painting," Karl reiterated. "The priceless Carson Desi you claim to have returned. It's nowhere on the premises."

Lacey felt breathless with panic. If the painting was missing, it poked a huge, massive hole in her story of having gone to the store to return it. At best, it made her look like a liar. At worst... well, at worst it put her right in the frame as Edwin's killer.

"Did you check behind all the paintings?" Lacey asked, growing frantic. "I told Edwin to reframe it and hide it."

"It's a crime scene," Superintendent Turner said simply. "Every inch of that place has been searched with a fine-tooth comb. Trust me. The painting is gone."

Lacey's legs felt suddenly weak. She grabbed the doorframe to steady herself.

Edwin had been killed for the painting—the painting she'd forced him to take back! The *Wilfordshire Weekly* news report must've tipped someone nefarious off to the existence of the priceless artwork and somehow they'd connected all the dots and ended up on Edwin's doorstep. It was all her fault. That sweet, humble man had met a grisly end because of her! Because she'd forced him to take back the painting.

"It's missing," Lacey whispered under her breath, her eyes scanning the floorboards as her mind churned.

"Missing," came the detective's sneering voice. "Stolen... Never returned in the first place."

Lacey's angry glare darted back up to him. She'd reached the end of her patience.

"Whatever you're insinuating, Karl," she said through her clenched jaw, "why don't you just come out and say it?"

Turner gave her a fake-coy shrug.

"We have one missing painting," he said, counting on his fingers as he spoke. "And one dead man. It's simple mathematics. One plus one makes..." He opened his arms wide, indicating that Lacey was the answer to his equation. "You."

Lacey narrowed her eyes with loathing. Superintendent Turner looked like he was thoroughly enjoying this. Relishing it, even. He'd accused her of many things in his time, but this one really hurt. Edwin was a dear old man. She'd never do anything to harm him. For Superintendent Turner to even entertain the thought of her as Edwin's killer—as shoe-horned as it was—brought waves of sadness crashing over her.

Just then, Lacey's attention was distracted by movement and lights in the distance. She squinted over Superintendent Turner's shoulder to see a convoy of cop cars crawling up the hillside toward her cottage.

As if this were the cue he'd been waiting for, Superintendent Turner reached into his pocket and produced a piece of paper. He held it out at arm's length, just an inch away from her nose, and grinned with malevolence.

"I have a warrant to search your property."

CHAPTER FOURTEEN

Lacey barely had time to register her shock before a stream of cops came trooping in through her front door. She squished herself against the door frame, tightening her bathrobe against her to preserve her modesty. As far as early morning wake-up calls went, being told a man was dead and she was a suspect in his murder was about as bad as they came. She'd never complain about Gina's bleating sheep again.

DCI Beth Lewis, Superintendent Turner's young partner, brought up the rear of the procession. Her honey-colored hair was twisted into a tight bun at the nape of her neck, giving her the air of a severe ballerina. Dark bags beneath her eyes told Lacey she'd also been woken up earlier than she'd expected this morning.

She stopped on the doorstep. "Morning, Lacey. Sorry for the early morning intrusion."

"Beth, this was nothing to do with me," Lacey said, desperately. "You know I'm not capable of killing someone, don't you?"

Beth wasn't exactly a friend, but the two women were on friendly terms. At the very least, when it came to these kinds of matters, Beth was more likely to see things eye to eye with Lacey, which was more than could be said for Superintendent Turner. If anyone would believe Lacey had nothing to do with Edwin's murder, and help her out of the tight spot she'd found herself in, it would be Beth.

But the female detective seemed unmoved by her outpouring.

"The evidence will speak for itself," she said, cryptically.

Lacey didn't like the sound of that. It gave her the creeping fear that Beth may actually be suspicious of her this time, too. Even Lacey had to admit the set-up looked damning for her. She was very likely the last person to see Edwin alive, which gave her the opportunity to commit the crime. The painting gave her the motive. And if even Beth, who was usually in her corner, could suspect she had the means, then she really was in trouble.

"In that case, help yourself," Lacey told her, feeling defeated. "I have nothing to hide."

Beth gave a single nod.

"Is Chester on a leash?" she asked, glancing down at the dog beside Lacey, sniffing eagerly at all the new smells the police had brought in with them. "You don't want to give Turner any reason to impound him."

"I'll put him in the garden," Lacey said, her shoulders slumping from the weight of everything. "Come on, boy."

She turned and headed down the corridor. Chester followed alongside her, looking up at her pensively as if wondering why she'd become so morose all of a sudden.

If only dogs could talk, Lacey thought. She could do with a supportive ear right about now.

She felt hollow as she entered the kitchen. Moving robotically, she went over to the back door and shooed Chester outside so he could play his favorite game: herding Gina's sheep.

"Do you want a coffee?" Lacey called over her shoulder as DCI Lewis entered in after her. "You look like I feel."

"I'd better not," Beth said. "Turner thinks it's inappropriate to accept drinks while executing a search warrant."

"I suppose it is," Lacey replied.

She set the coffee machine up, and was about to choose her usual espresso, but decided, knowing Superintendent Turner as she did, he would be on some kind of crusade to prove her guilt and would take quite some time, so she may as well take a long coffee break. She selected the latte setting instead.

"Did Turner tell you about your store?" Beth Lewis said from the doorway where she was hovering.

Lacey swirled to face her, panicked. "What? No. What about my store?"

Beth looked a little uncomfortable. "It was searched this morning."

"What?" Lacey cried.

"Your store," Beth echoed. "Turner executed an early morning warrant."

Lacey was baffled. "While I was asleep? Surely that's illegal!"

"We were let in voluntarily," Beth admitted. She checked her notepad. "By a ... Finnbar Clarke."

Lacey let out a long, frustrated breath. Finnbar. Of course.

"He's only been working for me for a few weeks," Lacey lamented. "How did Karl even know where to find him?"

"You know what he's like," Beth mumbled, clearly awkward about her gung-ho partner's actions. "When he fixates on a theory it can be

67

nigh-on impossible to change his mind. And he's not exactly the sort of guy people refuse, is he?"

She could say that again. Lacey had had enough dealings with Karl Turner now to hold her own, but she could easily see how an anxious-prone guy like Finnbar would feel so intimidated he'd "voluntarily" let him into the store. Really, it was Lacey's mistake for giving him a set of keys. It was too much responsibility, too soon, and she'd left an easy in for Superintendent Turner to exploit. Gina had even challenged her over it. She should listen to her friend more.

"And all this at the crack of dawn?" Lacey said wryly. "I never took Karl for an early riser."

Beth clearly couldn't help herself. A smile flitted across her lips. But it was gone as soon as it had appeared.

"They're not going to find anything," Lacey added, trying to plead her case to the only person likely to listen. "I returned the painting to Chumley's yesterday. I'm a witness, not a suspect. You guys are wasting your time here. The actual killer is out there somewhere."

She gestured to the window, then had to grasp hold of the countertop. She couldn't believe this was happening. She took deep breaths, trying to soothe her mounting distress.

The coffee machine began making a throthing noise. Lacey was relieved for the distraction. She went over to finish off her latte.

"Sure you don't want one?" she asked.

There was no response. She turned around to discover the female officer was no longer there.

Lacey sighed and took her coffee over to the kitchen table. She sat, crossing one leg over the other, and watched through the window as Chester zigzagged back and forth across the garden, listening to the sound of the officers' footsteps as they stomped and thudded their way through her property.

Lacey sipped her coffee and thought about Edwin.

Dead. It just didn't seem real. She'd seen him just yesterday. He was old, yes, and frail, to an extent. But he was obviously fighting fit and had years left in him. The thought of someone springing up on that lovely, kind old man and harming him made her feel sick.

And for what? For a painting? It was too callous for words.

Suddenly, Lacey's coffee tasted too sweet, too sickly. She pushed it away, no longer able to stomach it.

Then she heard the sound of footsteps trudging downstairs. The police must've finished their fingertip search of her home. By the sounds of things, the team of officers were congregating by the front door in her low-ceilinged corridor. Lacey craned to overhear their conversation, even though she was quite confident about what the verdict would be.

"Nothing," a male voice said.

"The store search came back clear too," added the recognizable voice of Beth Lewis.

A few more muffled, indecipherable statements were exchanged, then Lacey heard the distinct sound of the front latch being opened and the police exiting.

I guess they're done, she thought, standing from the kitchen table and arranging her bathrobe to maintain her modesty. Or at least as much modesty as one could manage when dressed in basically a negligée.

The formidable figure of Superintendent Turner appeared in the kitchen doorway. He was built like a rugby player, large and wide-set enough to take up the whole space. In the time Lacey had known him, he'd gone fully gray. It always seemed to happen that way with the men who kept their hair instead of balding. One minute it was colored, the next, completely gray. It made him look like an angry polar bear.

"All done?" Lacey asked, using the same tone she would if asking a toddler whether they'd finished going potty.

"Our searches are complete," he replied with a stiff nod.

He was practically vibrating with frustration. It was quite obvious to Lacey that he was annoyed his hunch about her being the thief had turned out to be wrong.

"What happens next?" Lacey asked.

"You're still the last person to have seen Edwin Cross alive," Turner replied, gruffly. "And you're still the person who discovered a rare, priceless, now missing artwork."

"Sounds to me like you're formulating a theory," Lacey said. "Why don't you run it by me, so I know what I'm up against this time?"

Superintendent Turner's nostrils flared with anger. Gone was his earlier arrogance. Of all the people Lacey had met in her life, Karl Turner was the one who hated being proved wrong the most. Which always made it easy to poke the bear.

Just as Lacey expected, the detective took the bait.

"I know you never returned the painting to Edwin," he blabbed. "You went to Chumley's store, sure, but not to return his painting. You went to make sure he couldn't claim to be its rightful owner."

69

"Huh," Lacey said. "And you have evidence to back up this wild accusation? Witnesses? CCTV? Incriminating phone records?"

The detective said nothing, but he didn't need to. His pinched expression said it all. He looked like he'd taken a bite into a lemon.

"I'll take that as a no," Lacey finished.

Superintendent Turner didn't move. He just stood there, filling up the doorway, looking down at Lacey with fury. She could hear his breathing—deep and ragged. He was obviously trying to get in the last word. He always did.

"Don't even think about leaving town," he said.

Then he turned and stormed out of the cottage, slamming the door behind him.

"I wouldn't dream of it," Lacey said, sadly, to the empty air.

CHAPTER FIFTEEN

It wasn't that much past opening time when Lacey pushed open the door to her store. Gina was already inside tidying up the mess the earlier police search had left behind.

At the sound of the bell, Boudica leapt out of her doggy bed and rushed up to Chester. Gina made her way to her feet and approached Lacey with a worried expression. Lacey had filled her in on all that morning's shenanigans via text message.

"How are you holding up, chicken?" Gina asked, softly, giving her arm an affectionate rub.

Lacey sighed wearily. She was utterly exhausted.

"Still in shock," she told her friend. "Right now, there's too much to process."

She glanced around sadly at the askew furniture and messed up displays. The place was in disarray thanks to the police search. Although Lacey suspected it wouldn't do much to put the customers off, the fact there'd been a police search in the first place would do that rather effectively enough. Lacey knew how the rumor mill worked in Wilfordshire. Until Edwin's murder was solved, everyone would give her store a wide berth.

As she looked about, she realized that Gina was alone in the store.

"Where's Finnbar?" she asked.

Gina glanced at the clock. "Probably on his way in. He's usually here by nine thirty."

"I have a feeling he won't be turning up for his shift today," Lacey said.

Gina looked confused. "Why? What makes you say that? He's usually reliable enough."

Lacey began tidying up the furniture, nudging the red velvet love seat back into place, before straightening up the nested coffee tables beside it.

"What makes me say that?" Lacey echoed. "How about him letting the cops in to execute a search warrant of my store without me being present?"

Gina grimaced. "I guess that is pretty bad."

71

"And yet somehow that's not even the worst thing he's done," Lacey said.

She took hold of one side of a bookcase. Gina grabbed the other. Together they heaved and lugged the heavy wooden shelves back into place.

"Him blabbing to the reporters about the painting when I'd expressly asked him not to led to an innocent man getting murdered," Lacey finished.

A wave of grief strangled out her voice.

"So you've decided Finnbar was the one to leak to the press?" Gina asked. "I'm off the hook, am I?"

Lacey recovered her composure and gave her a look. "There were only three people here when I found the Carson Desi painting. *I* didn't call Annabella Josher with a tip. Did you?"

Gina shook her head. "Of course not."

"Well then," Lacey said, "through a simple process of elimination, we come up with our culprit."

They began maneuvering a smoke-glass-topped retro '70s dining table back into position.

"What I don't understand is why he'd even do that in the first place?" Gina wondered aloud. "You told him not to. And you made it pretty clear you'd be returning the painting to its owner anyway."

Lacey shrugged. "I don't know. Why does Finnbar do any of the things he does? He's an odd one."

Gina looked contemplative. "Let's say for argument's sake it was Finnbar who contacted the press. What makes you so sure the tip-off led to the murder?"

Lacey's throat clenched, just as it did every time she was reminded of the sweet antiques store owner who'd been so unfairly killed.

"It seems pretty clear cut to me," Lacey said. "Whoever killed Edwin did it to get the painting."

Gina shivered. "That's chilling. The depths some people descend to. Do you have any ideas who it might be?"

Lacey really wished she could say she'd drawn a blank. But the sad truth was, she hadn't. There *was* someone she was suspicious of. Someone she felt personally responsible for having brought into this whole thing in the first place.

"Finnbar," she announced.

Gina laughed. But when Lacey remained stony-faced, she stopped.

"Finn?" she exclaimed, sounding dumbfounded. "That poor boy doesn't know his arse from his elbow! How do you think he'd manage to kill someone? Even a blow to the head requires some degree of hand-eye coordination, something our peculiar little friend lacks."

"Gina, please," Lacey said.

She wasn't in the right frame of mind for Gina's particular brand of gallows humor.

"I'm being serious," Gina told her. "Finn isn't a killer. As much as he drives me batty, he's not the type."

"And what is the type?" Lacey challenged. "Looks can be deceiving. And if you think about it, it's the only scenario that makes sense. Finnbar knew who Carson Desi was right away. He was practically drooling at the sight of the painting. What if that whole tip-off to the reporters was to make sure all the suspicion was on me?"

Gina shook her head. She clearly wasn't buying it. "Well, first of all, it would've been easier to steal the painting directly off you, wouldn't it?"

"I disagree," Lacey said. "Stealing it from me would make it way too obvious it was him. Stealing it from Edwin's store after it had been returned at least opened up a whole load of different possibilities. Because technically anyone else who'd seen that news report could be culpable."

Gina held up a finger to stop her. "Except no one knew it came from Chumley's, did they? You never told Annabella Josher where the painting had come from, or where you'd returned it to. The painting was never linked to Edwin Cross's store at all, at least not explicitly."

Lacey paused for thought. It was a good point. She tried to cast her mind back to the night she'd brought the tomato painting into the store and discovered the Carson Desi behind it, when it had just been the three of them. Had she told them where she'd purchased the tomato painting from in the first place? She vaguely recalled having mentioned diverting because of a flood. And she'd also said that the store was in a converted barn. It wouldn't take a genius to check local weather reports for localized flooding and then use a map app to find the nearest antiques store. Finnbar was certainly smart enough to put two and two together.

"I think he worked it out," Lacey said.

Gina didn't look convinced. She folded her arms. "In that case, what are you intending to do about it?"

Lacey took a deep breath. "I'm going to speak to him. I can't leave the investigation up to Superintendent Turner. He loathes me. And anyway, I hate the idea of some thief profiting off the Carson Desi. Edwin wanted me to keep it after all. I had to twist his arm to get him to accept it back. He didn't want it, or the money, or the hassle that came with it..."

Her voice trailed away as she began to choke up again. It was almost as if the old man knew what kind of hassle the painting might bring him. If only she'd listened to him rather than forcing the painting back on him, he wouldn't have been killed.

Then a new, terrible thought hit Lacey. If she'd kept the painting, would she be the one now lying in a morgue? Would she have been murdered instead?

Lacey felt more compelled than ever to solve Edwin's murder.

CHAPTER SIXTEEN

Lacey crossed the street toward the patisserie, Chester trotting beside her. She'd barely spoken to Tom since they'd parted ways after their trip. She felt reluctant to fill him in on the case, but she knew he would worry otherwise, and it wasn't fair to cause him anxiety.

The bunting that zigzagged between the lamp posts had been changed for autumn, with oranges and reds to match the leaves of the turning trees. Tom's famous macaron window display had also been updated for the new season. Gone was the summer's rushed attempt at a racehorse (which had ended up looking tragically like a donkey), and in its place was a huge macaron jack-o'-lantern. Usually Lacey would love all the changes—the coolness in the air, the darker evenings, the crunchy, colorful leaves, all the things that told her fall was coming—but she was so stressed and wrapped up in Edwin's death, she could barely even raise a smile.

She entered the patisserie. The gorgeous, comforting aroma of gingerbread greeted her. Along with the window display, Tom liked to change the shape of his beloved gingerbread cookies to reflect the seasons and special events of the year. The smell meant he was back in the kitchen, busily experimenting with new cuts and designs.

Lacey and Chester wove through the tables—which were full, as always, with happy customers enjoying Tom's exceptional pastries—and up to the counter. Emmanuel, Tom's new assistant, was manning the till today. The dark-skinned young man was tall and lithe, and his white apron matched the pearly white of his teeth. He flashed Lacey one of his warm, welcoming smiles as she approached.

"Tom's in the kitchen," he said in his lilting Kenyan accent.

Lacey gave him a nod of thanks and headed through the arch into the kitchen.

As predicted, Tom was indeed in the middle of gingerbread experimentation. But instead of making cookies, he was sitting cross-legged on the floor constructing what appeared to be an entire gingerbread castle. It was at least as big as a child, and Tom was holding a piping bag in one hand, using the frosting like cement to stick the pieces of his castle together.

Chester bounded up to Tom and greeted him with a huge lick on the cheek. Tom started to laugh and almost lost his balance. He petted Chester in a rough-and-tumble way until the dog backed off. Then he looked up, searching for Lacey. When he found her, his eyes lit up.

"Hello fiancée!" he exclaimed.

Lacey shifted uncomfortably, realizing she still wasn't over the disaster of their Brighton trip.

"What is that monstrosity?" she asked.

Tom looked back at the half-formed structure. "This is going to be a haunted castle when I'm finished. I saw this amazing thing online, where you use a projector to make it look like there's a ghost inside a dollhouse. I figured I could try making my own version out of gingerbread."

When Lacey stayed silent, Tom uncrossed his legs and stood, his expression now serious.

"Is everything okay with you?" he asked.

"You heard about the painting?"

Tom nodded. "I watched it on the news. And also from the window."

Lacey cringed as she thought of the big white TV van that had been parked outside her store, and the reporter with her cameraman, mic, and boom. Pretty much every store on the high street had had a front row seat to the action. And she knew that every single one of them would be coming up with a theory about the discovery of the priceless Carson Desi and the murder of Edwin Cross, one that likely cast her as the villain. She knew she shouldn't let hearsay get to her, but the thought still troubled her.

"Did you hear about what happened to Edwin?" she asked, her voice wavering.

Tom nodded again. "Gina texted me. I'm really sorry."

He didn't ask why Lacey hadn't texted him herself, and Lacey was silently grateful he wasn't grilling her about it while she was in mourning.

She flashed him a sad smile. "I have a question. What time did you start work today?"

"It was an early one," Tom told her. "Five."

Five. Well before Superintendent Turner appeared on her doorstep to execute his search warrant.

"Why?" he added.

"Did you see the police come to my store?" Lacey asked.

"No. I was already in the kitchen by then."

"Damn. Okay."

She'd been hoping Tom had seen Finnbar. But it seemed not.

Just then, Tom put his hands on her shoulders and gave her a serious look.

"Lacey. Please tell me you're not going to try and investigate this yourself," he said.

Lacey kept her gaze steady on his green eyes. She knew what Tom wanted to hear, and she knew she couldn't give it to him.

"I can't promise that," she said, boldly.

Tom stepped back, letting his hands fall, and sighed.

"Why do you always do this?" he said, shaking his head. "Inject yourself into these situations?"

"Because I care about finding out the truth," Lacey told him. "And I care about not having my reputation in this town trashed over fake rumors and gossip."

Tom's gaze roved over her face. He looked agonized.

"Just be careful," he said. "I couldn't bear anything happening to you."

Lacey gave him a sad smile. "Nothing will happen to me. I promise." She looked over at Chester by the door. "I have my guard dog, don't I?"

She knew Tom was just looking out for her, but she didn't need protecting. She could hold her own.

"Fine," Tom said, accepting defeat. "But if you're going to play sleuth, you'd better keep me in the loop. Who's your prime suspect?"

"Finnbar," Lacey said.

Tom's eyebrows shot up. "That's... unexpected. Why him?"

"He was the only other person there except for Gina when I discovered the Carson Desi painting. In fact, he was the one to identify it. You should've seen him. He was practically salivating over it."

"Wouldn't you be, if you thought a super famous painting that had been lost to time was suddenly in your possession? Finnbar's a kook. A nerd. He's not a killer."

"That's what Gina said."

"Maybe you should listen to Gina," Tom said with a shrug. "I mean, I saw Finnbar this morning and he was perfectly normal. Normal for him, I mean. He wasn't acting like someone who'd just committed murder and theft."

Lacey straightened to alert. "You saw him? When?"

"He came in this morning to buy breakfast, like a minute after I arrived. Coffee and a croissant. I was surprised. He's never bought anything from me before."

Lacey's mind started turning over. Finnbar was a creature of habit. Tom had never served him coffee and croissants before because that wasn't what he had for breakfast. He ate breakfast at home, then had a pot of tea when he got to the store. For him to come into Tom's shop was unusual. Maybe he wasn't acting like someone who'd just committed murder and theft in a way anyone who didn't know him would recognize, but any change in habit could be a red flag.

"Did he say anything to you?" Lacey asked, her suspicions mounting.

Tom gave a nonchalant shrug. "Sure. I mean he was being pretty chatty. Asking all about our trip away. Where we'd been. How we'd ended up finding the antiques store in the first place. That sort of thing."

Lacey's suspicions piqued.

Finnbar, who was usually so socially awkward, had been making small talk with Tom. Very specific small talk about their trip...

What had he wanted that information for? To find his way to Chumley's so he could commit theft and murder?

It was a leap, Lacey knew. But it was the best theory she had so far.

She had to speak to Finnbar. She just had to find him first.

CHAPTER SEVENTEEN

Lacey hurried back into the store, passing Gina and heading straight into the office. She pulled open the top drawer of her filing cabinet and found the manila folder that was technically her entire HR department. Inside was Finnbar's job application, along with his references, emergency contact telephone numbers, and address.

She was surprised to see that Finnbar lived in one of Wilfordshire's quiet suburbs. Then she remembered that he still lived with his parents. Like most PhD students, he didn't earn enough cash through his part-time work to afford the luxury of his own apartment.

Lacey scribbled the address down on a sticky note, then locked her files back away. She went back into the store, Chester following along behind her.

"Where are you going?" Gina asked, hands on hips.

"To see if I can locate our AWOL shop assistant," she said.

She left the store before Gina could protest, and hopped into her champagne-colored Volvo. The weather was still warmer than it ought to be for late September, so she cracked the window. Chester put his nose to it, letting the breeze flutter through his ears as Lacey drove to the suburbs.

England's post-war developments tended to all look very similar— neat rows of red brick houses with white window frames and gray-slate roofs. Well-proportioned grassy gardens out front next to silver cars parked on brick-patterned driveways. Only their doors were different, painted an array of different colors, with different styles and numbers.

She parked beside the curb and ushered Chester out of the car, locking it behind her. Then she opened the wrought iron gate and went up to the shiny red door of Finnbar's parents' home.

Chester sat patiently on the step beside her as she took the brass door and rapped loudly three times.

There was no answer.

Lacey was ninety-nine percent sure Finnbar was inside somewhere. If he was playing hooky from work, where else would he be? She doubted he'd risk heading to the library or traveling to the university where his chances of being spotted by someone would be high.

Lacey crouched down and lifted the flap of the letter box. It squeaked, making Chester whine with curiosity.

Lacey peered through the slit. The house was neat, decorated in that typical middle-class way most English houses were—cream walls and matching rug, polished floorboards, family photos on a wooden dresser at the side, a coat rack with several coats hanging from the hooks. Lacey couldn't quite picture scruffy Finnbar coming from this overly organized, somewhat stale home environment.

She knocked again, the sharp *rat-a-tat* noise echoing around the corridor.

This time, Lacey heard a noise. It came from one of the rooms off to the side and sounded distinctly like someone stumbling.

Though Lacey couldn't quite see from this vantage point, she didn't need to know Finnbar was there, hiding just out of sight. Knowing him, he'd tripped over his own feet in his haste to avoid her spotting him through the letterbox.

"Finnbar! I know you're in there!" Lacey yelled through the letterbox. "Answer the door! I'm your boss and I order you to open the door!"

Nothing.

Lacey had no choice but to pull out the big guns.

"If you don't answer this door right now I'll fire you!" she yelled.

There was a moment of stillness, then Finnbar's scruffy brown brogues came striding into her line of sight. He was coming for the door. Lacey let go of the letterbox flap and it pinged back into place.

She straightened to standing at the same time the door was opened from the inside. And there stood Finnbar. Plaid shirt. Beige slacks. Just the same as every other day.

"Good morning, Lacey," Finnbar said, tipping his imaginary cap. "Chester."

He petted the dog's head, just like he did every day. He was clearly trying his best to play this whole thing off as nothing.

Lacey cut right to the chase.

"Good morning?" she said. "Good morning? I'll tell you what's a good morning for me—not having the police crawling through my home and business premises. What the hell happened? How did you end up letting the police into my store?"

Finnbar, usually so anxious, managed to maintain his composure. "They had a warrant. I didn't think I was allowed to refuse."

Lacey sucked air between her teeth. It was as she'd expected, and she couldn't exactly fault him. When confronted by the opposing figure of Superintendent Turner, a young, inexperienced man like Finnbar would be bound to cave.

"Why were you up so early in the first place?" Lacey asked. "They were there at six a.m.!"

"I always wake up early."

Lacey narrowed her eyes. "Really? And you always buy a coffee and croissant from Tom at five a.m. too, do you?"

Finnbar shifted uncomfortably. Now she had him.

"Lacey, what are you accusing me of?" he asked.

Lacey felt the emotion rising through her, reaching a boiling point. "I want to know why you were drilling Tom for information about the antiques store. Did you want to know where it was so you could go and steal the painting? Finnbar, did you kill Edwin?"

She hadn't meant to just turn up at his door and accuse him outright, but now she was face to face with him, all her emotion spilled out and she just couldn't hold back.

Finnbar looked appalled. "How can you even think that? How can you even think I might be capable of..." He looked past her into the street, his gaze darting back and forth as he checked for eavesdroppers, before finishing, in a whisper, "murder?"

"Tell me I'm wrong," Lacey challenged. "Tell me why you were at the store so early this morning."

Finnbar looked flustered. "I went to the store because the cops told me I had to let them in! But before that, I went into the patisserie because it was the only place open that early. I bought a coffee because I was tired. I had a hard time sleeping last night, and you're always going on about how brilliant coffee is first thing in the morning. My parents aren't coffee drinkers so there was none in the house. But it was way too strong for me and I got all jittery, so I brought a croissant to try and soak up some of the caffeine."

Lacey frowned. She was pretty sure caffeine couldn't be soaked up with food like alcohol could, but it was the sort of thing she could easily imagine Finnbar thinking.

"Why were you trying to trick Tom into telling you where the antiques store was?" she challenged.

"I wasn't," Finnbar said. "I was talking to him because the coffee made me hyper. I remembered you'd been away so it was the first thing that popped into my head to talk about. There's nothing more to it. I wasn't trying to trick him, and I wasn't trying to find out where the antiques store was either. After I left the patisserie I walked around the high street trying to work off the excess energy. That's what I was doing when that superintendent guy found me and demanded I let him into the store. One of the officers that was with him is my parents' neighbor, and he recognized me walking around, so they didn't need to go to my house. Later, when the police were done, I locked up the store again and came home to watch my breakfast news show. I don't like missing it."

Lacey twisted her lips. Either Finnbar was really good at lying, or his story was starting to add up.

She studied him with her eyes, not sure how much, if any, of his story she should swallow. He certainly had an answer for everything, even if it was a strange and convoluted one. But knowing Finnbar as she did, none of it actually seemed that far out of the realm of his normal.

"Why did you miss your shift this morning?" Lacey asked, changing lanes.

Not turning up to work was pretty incriminating in Lacey's opinion, especially for someone who usually ran like clockwork.

"Because when I spoke to my parents this morning and told them what happened, they told me I shouldn't have let the police in without you present," Finnbar said. "I thought you were going to be mad at me. And since you're already mad at me because of all that broken crockery, and the press—who I didn't tip off, I promise you—I guess I was too scared to see you. And then I got to thinking that maybe you were the killer…"

"Me?" Lacey cried. Now it was her turn to look appalled. "What made you think that?"

He shrugged. "I don't know. I don't really know you that well, I suppose. You're kind of scary when you want to be."

Lacey let out a huge breath. What a mess this was turning into, with each of them suspicious of the other. And while they were here bickering and pointing the finger at one another, some evil person was out there getting away with murder!

"I'm sorry, Finnbar," Lacey said, finally deciding she'd been barking up the wrong tree with this one.

Finnbar wedged his shoulder against the doorframe. "That's okay. But I'm curious. When exactly did you think I'd have time to kill the antiques man? I only spoke to Tom about your trip this morning. And then it was only about ten minutes after I even knew where Chumley's was located that the police were already executing their search warrant."

It was a good point. For Finnbar to be the killer, he would have obviously needed to have gone to Chumley's before the body was found this morning. But if he only knew where it was because of the information he'd gotten from Tom, there wouldn't have been time.

She remembered then how she'd worked out he might have put all the puzzle pieces together from scraps of information she'd revealed the night they'd found the Carson Desi in the first place. He wouldn't have needed information from Tom, after all, just a weather report and a map of the local area.

He still had time to commit the crime.

Lacey realized she'd been too hasty in letting Finnbar off the hook. She needed to question him some more.

"Were you home all night?" Lacey asked, slipping straight back into detective-mode.

Finnbar nodded. "There was a special episode of *Space Voyage X* on. Double-bill. It's my favorite TV show. I've seen every episode. I was on the forum talking about it with the other Voyagers all night. That's what us fans call ourselves."

Unsurprisingly, of all the things Finnbar had told her so far, this was the one she fully believed.

"Why?" he asked. Then a little frown appeared between his brows. "Oh. You still suspect me."

Lacey shook her head. "I don't. I'm sorry."

She was finally ready to accept she'd been wrong about Finnbar. In fact, she felt pretty foolish for having questioned him in the first place.

"Phew," Finnbar said, wiping his brow. "Because I promise you I had nothing to do with anything. I didn't tip off the press either."

"The verdict's still out on that one," Lacey told him, narrowing her eyes.

She wasn't about to let him off the hook for everything, and there was no other explanation for how they'd found out.

Just then, Lacey felt her phone vibrating in her pocket.

"Back in a sec," she said to Finnbar, turning and stepping off his doorstep.

She grabbed her phone, expecting it to be the police. Instead, the word *Mom* flashed up at her.

"Crap!" Lacey exclaimed.

This was about the absolute worst time her mother could call, right when she was in the middle of trying to solve a murder. But avoiding her mom was never a good idea.

So with bated breath, Lacey answered the call.

CHAPTER EIGHTEEN

Chester followed Lacey back along Finnbar's garden path as she put the cell phone to her ear.

"Hi, Mom," she said, stepping onto the sidewalk and stopping beside a silver hatchback, one of several identical cars parked along the curb outside the Identi-Kit houses. "Is everything okay?"

"Yes, of course everything is okay," Shirley replied. "Why do you always have to ask if everything is okay? I'm just calling to catch up."

Typical Shirley. Always on the combative. Never bothering with the usual pleasantries. Never even attempting to be pleasant in the first place.

Lacey took a deep breath to calm herself, and focused on a row of ants marching back and forth between a weed growing out a crack in the asphalt next to the metal storm drain.

"Sorry, Mom," she said. "How is everything with you?"

Shirley promptly ignored the question. "Have you set a date for the wedding yet?"

Wedding? Lacey thought.

The word sounded alien to her. She'd barely given her upcoming nuptials a thought since she'd returned from her trip. She was supposed to be knee-deep in wedding preparations! Instead, she was knee-deep in a murder investigation.

"Not yet," she told her mom.

"Well, how long will it be?" Shirley demanded. "I want a good deal on the flights and if you leave it to the last minute the prices will shoot up."

Lacey felt her heart rate increase as her mom's questions forced her to think about her father, and how she'd lost him all over again in Rye. Possibly for good.

"I won't leave it until the last minute in that case," Lacey told her, stiffly.

"Don't be a smart-aleck," Shirley said with a sigh.

"I'm not trying to be," Lacey said, apologetically. "I just have a lot on my mind right now."

A murder investigation. A lost father. A missing painting. A lot was an understatement.

"Well, have you looked at any venues yet?" Shirley continued, in the same interrogative tone.

No wonder Lacey's pulse always spiked whenever her mom was on the line. She always put her on the spot, and forced her to think about terrible things she wasn't able to talk about aloud.

"Not yet," Lacey told her, trying her best to sound breezy.

"Good," Shirley said. "I want to be there when you do."

Lacey tensed. The last thing she could cope with right now was her mom visiting from the States!

"Mom, that's very sweet of you to want to be involved," Lacey said, cautiously, "but I'm honestly nowhere near deciding anything. I don't know if it will be a summer, spring, or fall wedding. I don't even know if it'll be within the year. So you don't have to stress out just yet."

"Who said I was stressing out?" Shirley retorted. Then there was a pause. When she spoke again, her voice sounded strangely childlike. "I just don't want to be left out again."

Lacey's heart clenched. Her mom's usual strategy for managing her emotions was to be combative and spikey. But it was the times when she let her vulnerability show that Lacey could actually see the situation from her point of view. Ever since Lacey had moved abroad, her mom had missed out on a whole bunch of important life events—opening the store, adopting Chester, buying Crag Cottage, and now her engagement to Tom. She was just sad about missing out on her elder daughter's life.

"How about this?" Lacey said, finally able to be diplomatic. "Any time I check out a venue or dress, I'll video call you to get your opinion on it."

There was a pause on the line. "Yes. Okay. I like that idea. Let's book something in now while I have you on the phone. Are you free Saturday?"

And just like that, Lacey's attempt to compromise with her mom backfired spectacularly. She could picture Shirley sitting in her New York apartment with her diary open on her knees, pen poised.

"I can't commit to anything right now," Lacey said.

"Why not?"

"I'm super busy."

"What with? What on earth could be more important than planning your wedding?"

It was a valid question. In an ideal world, nothing would be more important to Lacey right now than planning her wedding. But this wasn't an ideal world. Instead of imagining white dresses and bouquets, Lacey's mind kept conjuring images of Edwin Cross lying dead in the morgue. Instead of obsessing over seating arrangements, she was obsessing about a missing Carson Desi painting and the thieving murderer who'd taken it. Instead of working out a guest list, she was wondering whether her father had even read her letter, or if he'd run away when he'd realized she'd found him, and was lost somewhere in the world, never to be found again.

Not that she was about to tell her mom any of that…

"Work stuff," she said, evasively.

"So you really haven't made any preparations?" Shirley queried. "I thought you were lying."

"I wouldn't lie to you, Mom," Lacey said, before remembering, seconds earlier, she had done just that. "I'm just taking my time."

"This isn't coming from Tom, is it?" Shirley asked. "He's not forcing you to have one of those long engagements, is he? Because I think that's very disrespectful. And it's a sign of a poor character to propose to a woman with no intentions of actually walking her down the aisle within the year."

"Mom…" Lacey said, gently. "We've only been engaged for a few weeks. And you love Tom. You know he's a decent man. This isn't pressure from him. It's me. I'm the one choosing to take it slow. Okay?"

Shirley fell quiet.

"Fine," she said at last. "Will you send me a picture of the engagement ring at least?"

This, Lacey could do. "Sure. Give me a second."

She moved the phone from her ear and switched it to camera mode. She positioned it over her left hand, where the beautiful rose-gold Edwardian antique engagement ring looked stunning on her ring finger. She was just about to snap a photo when a sudden thought hit her.

Engagement ring!

There had been a man at Chumley's trying to sell his engagement ring when she'd bought the painting: the driver of the red Jeep Cherokee. He'd seen her buying the tomato painting, because he'd bumped right into her on his way out of the store. What if he'd seen her on the news report? He could've put two and two together and driven back to Chumley's to steal the painting. He certainly seemed like a pushy bully. In the short amount of time Lacey had been in his company, he'd proven himself to be both rude and aggressive.

Finally, Lacey had a new lead to pursue. She had a potential suspect.

"Lacey?" came Shirley's distant tinny voice through the cell phone. "Lacey, are you still there?"

Lacey suddenly remembered what she was supposed to be doing. She snapped the photo of her ring and sent it over to her mom, then put the phone back to her ear.

"Sorry, I was trying to get better lighting," she lied. "Did the picture arrive?"

"Oh. Oh Lacey," came Shirley's choked up voice. "That's really very beautiful."

Lacey was touched. She and her mom rarely shared the same taste in anything, especially when it came to antiques. Antiquing had been her father's business and passion, after all, so by default Shirley disliked anything to do with it. She wasn't one for being level-headed about things like that.

"Thank you," Lacey said. "Tom knows me well."

"He does," Shirley said with a hitch in her voice. "You're very lucky to have found one another."

"Oh, Mom," Lacey said, moved to hear her mom getting emotional. It wasn't often Shirley let her soft side show.

"Promise me not to leave me out of any of the preparations, okay?" Shirley asked.

"I promise," Lacey said. Then thinking again of Edwin Cross, whose life had been stolen from him so cruelly and so suddenly, she added, "I love you."

"I love you too, darling."

The call ended. For a brief moment, Lacey let herself bask in the touching moment she'd shared with her mom.

Then she put her cell phone away. She had a suspect to chase.

CHAPTER NINETEEN

Lacey walked back up the garden path to Finnbar's front door. He'd been standing there the whole time she'd been on the phone with her mom, waiting like an obedient school child for his teacher to dismiss him from class. Lacey felt kind of bad for having pulled the boss card on him earlier, threatening to fire him through the letterbox. It hadn't been her finest moment. She could see what he meant by her being scary sometimes. She'd have to work on that.

Finnbar looked up as she approached.

"Is everything okay?" he asked.

"Just my mom," Lacey said, shoving her phone away in her jeans pocket. "Hey, you're smart, aren't you?"

Finnbar frowned. "I mean, I'm doing a PhD. So, yeah. I guess."

He looked suspicious of her intentions. Which was fair enough, Lacey thought. Moments ago she'd been accusing him of being a murderer, now she was flattering him.

"Do you think you could help me with something computery?" she asked.

Lacey herself was absolutely woeful at anything to do with technology. If she never had to look at another computer screen again in her life that would be perfectly fine with her.

"Depends," Finnbar said. "What do you need done? I can't do any computer programming or anything like that."

Lacey shook her head. "No. Nothing that in-depth. I just need some help tracking someone down."

Finnbar narrowed his eyes. "A suspect?"

Lacey hesitated. It hadn't been her intention to get Finnbar caught up in her sleuthing. But now she had, she may as well be honest. "Could be."

Finnbar shrugged. "I can give it a go. Anything to clear my name."

He flashed her a sheepish look as he moved away from the door and beckoned Lacey inside.

She stepped into his parents' neat home, catching a smell of lavender. It was immaculately clean, the sort of cleanliness only someone without a pet could ever achieve.

"Am I allowed to bring Chester inside?" she asked. "He's shedding."

"It's fine," Finnbar said. "Mom hoovers twice a day."

He was already halfway down the corridor. Lacey shrugged and beckoned her dog inside, then shut the door after her.

She followed Finnbar into a small downstairs study. It had honey-colored floorboards, polished to perfection, bookshelves filled with intimidatingly thick textbooks, and a row of different types of guitars in stands.

"Do you play?" Lacey asked Finnbar.

"They're my dad's," he said, sitting in a swivel chair. "He uses this room like a studio."

He fired up the computer and typed in his log-in details.

Lacey lowered herself on the couch next to him, which was a futon folded up into sofa position. The family probably used the study as a guest room when Finnbar's dad wasn't busy rocking out in it.

Chester leapt up beside her, turned a few circles to get comfy, then flopped down and dropped his head into her lap.

"So what do you need me to do?" Finnbar asked.

Lacey petted Chester's silky fur as she spoke. "The other day at Chumley's, there was a guy trying to sell Edwin an engagement ring. He was being really aggressive about it. Really pushy. He's the only other person besides you, me, Tom, and Gina who knows where I bought a painting that day. I'm wondering if he heard about the discovery of the Carson Desi and worked out it was me who'd found it."

Finnbar's eyebrows rose. "That sounds promising."

"That's what I thought. But it could be nothing. I figured if we checked online listings of people selling engagement rings, we might stand a chance of tracking him down that way."

"Not a bad idea," Finnbar said, turning back to the computer and typing.

Lacey watched as he pulled up a bunch of different websites for reselling secondhand objects and typed *engagement ring* into the search box. He hit enter and thousands of hits appeared on the screen.

"I'll narrow it down to the local area," Finnbar said, clicking on a filter.

But even with the filter in place there were still hundreds of ads for secondhand rings.

"Looks like a lot of folks don't make it beyond the engagement stage," Finnbar commented. "Do any of these look familiar to you?"

Lacey glanced over his shoulder at the reams of photos. She hadn't gotten a particularly clear view of the ring when she'd been in the store. Beyond the man insisting it was twenty-four-karat gold, she had little else to go on.

"No," she said.

She sank back into the futon chair, frustrated.

Finnbar spun around. "Anything else we might be able to use to trace him down?"

Lacey clicked her fingers. "He was driving a red Jeep Cherokee! Tom said you don't see many of them in this country."

Finnbar looked excited. "He's right. We can use that."

He opened a new window and began filling the search bar with different combinations of phrases relating to engagement rings and Jeep Cherokees. After a while, he pulled up a social media profile. The profile was mainly private, with just a few updates going back over the years, for special life events.

Gaz and Maria - engaged! one of them read. Not too far below that was the update: *Treated myself to this little beaut!* along with a photo of a red Jeep Cherokee. Resting against its hood was none other than the man from Chumley's.

"I—I don't believe it," Lacey stammered. "That's him! How did you do that?"

"People have no idea how much revealing stuff they've actually put about themselves online," Finnbar told her. "Even when you have your settings on private, a whole bunch of stuff slips through."

"Good thing I'm such a technophobe," Lacey said.

She peered at the screen, narrowing her eyes as she took in Gaz's appearance.

Did you kill Edwin? Lacey thought.

"Whoa," Finnbar said then, breaking through her thoughts. "Check this out. Gaz works at the local news station."

Lacey blinked, shocked. "What?"

Finnbar pointed excitedly to the screen. "It says right here: Gaz Baker—video editor at *Wilfordshire Weekly* on Your TV."

Lacey was stunned. "Gaz definitely would've seen Annabella Josher's news report, in that case. He totally would've recognized me from Chumley's, and worked out that's where I'd taken the painting back to."

91

Suddenly, all arrows were pointing at Gaz Baker as Edwin's murderer and the thief of the painting. For the first time, Lacey had a truly compelling suspect.

"What are you going to do?" Finnbar asked. "Confront him? Their editing studios are in Exeter. I could find the address if you wanted to drive up there."

Lacey shook her head, remembering Superintendent Turner's instructions. "I can't leave town. The cops will arrest me if I do." She paused and thought it through. "How about this? We message him pretending to be interested in buying the engagement ring?"

"Sure," Finnbar said. "But how will you lure him to Wilfordshire? Not many people want to travel for an hour on the off chance they'll be able to make a sale."

"I have an idea," Lacey said. "I can tell him I think the ring might be worth a lot of money and that I'd like to value it."

"Cunning," Finnbar said. He turned back to the computer and typed a message. "How does this sound? *'Dear Mr. Baker, I'm an antiquer who's interested in valuing your engagement ring, as I believe it may be a rare piece from a discontinued line.'*"

Lacey was impressed. "That's perfect. Send it."

Finnbar did as he was commanded. Then he turned in his chair to face Lacey.

"Do you really think this guy might've done it?" he said.

"There certainly seem to be a lot of things pointing to him," Lacey replied, shuddering at the thought of the man on the computer screen lounging against his Jeep Cherokee striking Edwin to death. "But I won't know until I'm face to face with him."

Just then, she heard a ding come from the computer.

"That'll be him," Finnbar said, turning back around.

"Already?" Lacey replied. "That was quick."

"He must be very eager to put Maria behind him," Finnbar said, his eyes scanning the screen. "He wants to meet today."

Lacey gulped. This was all going very fast. Much faster than she'd expected. But the quicker she could solve this thing and clear her name, the better.

"Tell him to come to the store," she told Finnbar.

Finnbar gave her a wary look. "Are you sure? Isn't that a bit dangerous? This guy may well be a murderer."

Lacey didn't need reminding of the danger she was putting herself in. She was well aware she was taking a huge personal risk. She petted Chester's head for comfort.

"I have my guard dog," she said as much to reassure herself as Finnbar.

"If you say so," Finnbar said, sounding thoroughly unconvinced.

He typed a reply message and sent it away. A moment later the confirmation pinged into his inbox. Lacey had an appointment with her prime suspect.

There was no backing out now.

CHAPTER TWENTY

Lacey drummed her fingers anxiously on the countertop in her store, her eyes fixed on the door.

As soon as she'd gotten back to the store from Finnbar's home, she'd sent Gina home. She didn't want her friend to give her a lecture about how risky a plan this was.

Just then, Lacey spotted the red Jeep Cherokee pull to a halt on the sidewalk. Out hopped the grumpy man who'd barged into her at Chumley's, back before sweet Edwin's life had been snuffed out.

Are you his killer? Lacey thought, shuddering.

The doorbell jangled as Gaz the Jeep man shoved it roughly open. Chester let out a low growl as the man stomped across the floorboards toward the counter.

Lacey showed Chester the palm of her hand, telling him to relax. His growling ceased, but his eyes remained alert as he followed the man's path toward Lacey.

"Lacey?" the Jeep man said.

"That's right," Lacey replied, keeping her voice breezy. "You're Gaz?"

He nodded. There wasn't even a hint of recognition in his eyes. Either he was masking it because he was guilty, or their brief encounter back at Chumley's had left no impression on him and he was innocent.

Still, Lacey noted the strange energy he had about him. It was a sort of shiftiness, like he was expecting someone to pounce on him from behind at any second. His movements were jerky. Hasty.

As he pulled the gold engagement ring out of his pocket, a bunch of lint came with it and sprayed over the countertop. He flung the ring down like it had absolutely no personal significance to him at all.

"You reckon this is worth something, huh?" he said in a gruff voice, making an unpleasant scritching noise as he ran a hand over the dark stubble on his chin.

Lacey took the ring, turning it in her fingers. It was a solid yellow gold band. She inspected it closely, partly to give off the pretense of examining it, but mostly to avoid meeting Gaz's eye. His shiftiness was putting her on edge. It didn't help that Chester looked like he was ready to bring him down at even a moment's provocation.

"I need to inspect it for defects," Lacey said. "It might be from a line that was discontinued due to a fault. They're starting to fetch a decent amount at auctions now. It's one of those silly things where the imperfect ones become more sought after. Like that Harry Potter novel with a misprint."

Gaz frowned. Harry Potter wasn't the way to go with him, Lacey noted.

"If I can make some dosh off it then my relationship won't have been a total bust," he murmured.

So far, he'd shown no interest in anything beyond getting as much money from the ring as possible.

Lacey reached for her loupe and inspected the ring through it. It was actually a pretty nice vintage ring, with a genuine hallmark and an inscription that confirmed its twenty-four-karat purity.

"Where did you buy this?" she asked, genuinely curious as to why such a rough-looking man would've proposed with a vintage ring, rather than a diamond-encrusted Tiffany ring which was the sought-after style among young women these days.

"Family heirloom," he said. "My pops was a builder. Salt of the earth bloke. Built himself up from the ground up, ya know. He told us all to put our spare cash into gold. Makes more interest than a bank. When he snuffed it, all his gold got dished out among us. Smart bloke, God rest his soul."

Lacey tried to read Gaz, to look for any telltale signs of him being a murderer. He seemed impatient, sure, and bitter about his failed engagement. He also seemed shifty and uncomfortable, but that could literally mean anything. But with everything added together, there were certainly enough red flags for Lacey to want to dig further and get more out of him. It was time to start needling him for more.

"Well, I can't find the defect," she said, looking up. "But that doesn't mean it's not worth anything. It's a great ring regardless." She placed it on the electronic weighing scales. "I suspect you've had a lot of interest in this."

Gaz scoffed. "Hardly. No one I've shown it to yet has even put in an offer."

"Curious," Lacey feigned. "Where have you tried?"

"Every single backwater hovel I've come across," Gaz said with a scoff.

"Backwater hovel?" Lacey echoed, forcing out a chuckle. "I suppose you mean Chumley's?"

Though it hurt her heart to ridicule Edwin's store like that, she knew she had to speak on Gaz's level if she wanted him to open up to her.

"The cowshed outside Exeter? Yeah, that's the one." He let out a noise of derision. "The bloke there was a proper muppet."

Lacey swallowed the lump in her throat.

"The owner has no idea what anything's worth," she said.

Her switch to the present tense was deliberate. If Gaz switched back to the past tense while discussing Edwin, it might indicate he already knew he was dead. Alternatively, it might merely indicate him innocently referring to an event that had taken place in the past.

As it was, Gaz said nothing at all. Lacey would have to keep kneading him to speak more.

"I bought a painting from there for five bucks," she continued, conversationally. "I'll be able to sell it on for thousands."

She wanted to see whether Gaz would admit to recognizing her, and admit he knew all about the situation with the tomato painting and the Carson Desi.

There was a moment of recognition in his eyes.

"Hey, I know you…" he said.

Lacey felt her adrenaline spike. "You do?"

"Yeah. I work at the news station. Were you a talking head the other day?" He clicked his fingers. "Yeah. I remember editing your sequence now. You found a lost dog or something? An old painting? What was it again? I edit so many of these things I lose track."

"It was a painting," Lacey offered.

"Huh," Gaz grunted.

The conversation stalled there. He wasn't giving anything else away. Lacey decided to take a risk.

"If you don't mind me asking," she said, "why are you selling the ring? If it's a family heirloom, don't you want to keep it?"

It was a risky move. Men like Gaz had a lot of pride. Being poor was not something they'd readily admit to.

He glowered at her. Lacey felt her heart race.

"The ex cleared me out," he finally said. "Emptied the safe and the bank accounts and hopped on a plane to Lanzarote to shack up with some barman. I had to sell all my chains just to pay the mortgage. Even sold my filling." He pointed at his tooth, which was sporting an ugly hole where a (presumably gold) filling used to be.

"I'm so sorry," Lacey said, simultaneously feeling bad for him and a bit grossed out by the sight of his cavity.

"I've been working flat out since Marie cleared me out. Had to take on a second job. I do my daytime editing for the *Wilfordshire Weekly*. Then I drive all the way to Penzance to nighttime edit for this awful reality dating show."

Lacey frowned with contemplation. Nighttime edit? In Penzance? Lacey might not be from England originally, but she'd lived here long enough to know the name of the famous town on its farthest most southwesterly tip. It was about a hundred miles away from Wilfordshire. For Gaz to have killed Edwin, he would have needed to first drive the hour northeast from Wilfordshire to Chumley's after his day shift, then all the way southwest, for a hundred miles or so, to Penzance in time for his nighttime shift. How would he have fit it all in?

"That sounds like a lot of work," Lacey said, digging for more.

"It is," Gaz replied. "I can't remember the last time I got a decent night's sleep. I've been doing this for weeks now."

Suddenly, Gaz was looking less and less like a suspect to Lacey. Having a motive and means meant nothing without the opportunity.

"Weeks?" she repeated, her eyebrows rising. It took all her focus to keep her voice level. "Your poor car. All that wear 'n' tear. You must be racking up a ton of mileage."

She was trying to play it off as curiosity, but actually she was just trying to encourage him to offer up yet more information. If Gaz had really been working his excessive pattern for weeks, then he couldn't be Edwin's killer.

"You can say that again," he said, grunting. "An extra thousand miles a week! It's gonna cost me an arm and a leg during my next MOT."

Lacey quickly did the calculation in her head. It checked out. He was being honest. Gaz wasn't the killer.

"Anyway, it'll be worth it once I'm back in the black," Gaz continued. "And once I've gotten rid of that thing…" he looked at the ring with distaste, "it'll be like Marie never happened. So, what can you offer me for that?"

Lacey hadn't been expecting to actually make an offer on the ring, but it was genuinely a pretty solid piece, well worth several hundred pounds. Even if she couldn't sell it in the store or at a future auction, Gaz's pops was right about gold making more interest than the bank. Maybe she'd keep it for herself.

"Five hundred," Lacey said, looking up at Gaz.

His eyes widened with a look of both surprise and relief.

"Good," he said, nodding. "Once that's gone, I can have a clean start."

"Then shall we shake on it?" Lacey said.

She reached her hand forward. Gaz shook it. Lacey took the opportunity to look for any cuts or scratches, any signs he might have recently wielded a weapon. There was nothing, just a letter tattooed over each of his knuckles, unfortunately spelling out the name "M-A-R-I-E."

Lacey was decided. It wasn't him. Gaz wasn't her man.

"I expect you'll be wanting that removed at some point," she said, as she opened up the till and began counting out bills.

Gaz looked at his knuckles. "Nah. The next one might be called Marie, too. Then I'll be laughing."

He rasped out a smoker's laugh. Lacey didn't find his joke particularly funny, but she chuckled politely.

They exchanged money and ring, and Gaz left.

As soon as he was gone, Chester relaxed, lay down in his basket, and slept.

Lacey wondered about Gaz. He wasn't the killer. He was just your average rough 'n' ready type trying to keep himself afloat after a bad break-up.

She was at a dead end again.

Just then, she heard a noise come from the back room of the store. Chester woke immediately, his ears pinging up. He began to bark feverishly.

There was someone there.

CHAPTER TWENTY ONE

Lacey crept anxiously toward the auction room. Chester stayed close to her heels, ever the protector.

When she reached the back room, she recognized the figure standing there, and all her fear left her body like an elastic band snapping.

"Taryn?" Lacey demanded. "What the hell are you doing back here?"

The boutique owner from next door was casually standing in her back room like she owned the place. Behind her, the French doors were standing open. Lacey remembered now that she'd opened them up in order to let the air circulate in this unseasonably hot weather. It hadn't occurred to her that her nemesis would take it as an open invitation.

"Did you hop over the fence?" Lacey asked, incredulously.

Taryn advanced. "We need to talk about the air-conditioning situation," she said, ignoring the question.

"Do we?" Lacey replied with exasperation. "I have a lot of other things to worry about right now. Besides, it's not like you need my approval, anyway. You're going to go ahead and bash holes through my wall whether I agree to it or not."

"I had no choice," Taryn said. "You never answered my email about the quote."

"You gave me less than a day…" Lacey began to argue, before stopping dead in her tracks. A thought had hit her so strongly and suddenly, it was like being hit by a freight train.

"The hole!" she cried, pointing a finger of accusation at Taryn. "You overhead us speaking through the hole! You're the one who called the *Wilfordshire Weekly* about the painting!"

Finally, it all made sense. Taryn must've been inside her boutique during the discovery of the Carson Desi painting. She'd overheard the whole thing. While Lacey was telling Finnbar in no uncertain terms not to call the reporters about it, Taryn was probably already dialing their number. It was exactly the sort of thing she'd do, just to shake things up and cause a nuisance.

"Well?" Lacey demanded. "Was it you?"

Taryn pursed her lips. It was obvious she'd been caught out and couldn't even think of an excuse.

"You did!" Lacey cried, snapping her fingers. "Taryn, why would you do such a thing? A man is dead because of you!"

Taryn pulled a face of disgust. "I don't think you can blame that on me."

"It was the tip-off to the press that brought the murderer to Edwin's door in the first place," Lacey challenged. "Just because you like to make my life more difficult, a man's been murdered. I hope you're happy with yourself."

"Get a grip," Taryn huffed. "It's not like I'm the one who bashed him over the head!"

"Aren't you?" Lacey shot back.

She knew Taryn wasn't the killer. Not really. The malnourished fashionista had next to no muscle mass. She wouldn't be able to attack a man if her life depended on it. But Lacey was so furious with her and her petty behavior she couldn't help but lash out. This time she'd taken it too far. When Taryn's shenanigans harmed Lacey, and Lacey alone, that was one thing. She could handle herself. But this time Taryn's blabbing had caused a man to die, and that Lacey just couldn't forgive.

Though accusing Taryn wouldn't get her anywhere, putting a bit of heat on the woman might make her feel a tiny bit better about it all.

"Now you've admitted to knowing about the painting, you've put yourself right in the frame as a suspect," Lacey said.

"Come off it," Taryn said, putting her hands on her bony hips.

"The police will want to talk to you," Lacey added.

"So what?" Taryn said. She wasn't easily flapped. "I had nothing to do with it."

Lacey suddenly remembered poor Finnbar, who she'd put all the blame on. She'd have to apologize to him next time she saw him.

"I accused Finnbar. I thought he'd betrayed me. But all along it was you."

Taryn grimaced. "Who cares? That boy is a weirdo. I don't know why you want him working here. Good riddance if you ask me."

"I didn't ask you!" Lacey snapped. "I don't even want you here."

She'd never truly lost her temper at Taryn. She was usually able to take the higher road. But this time it was personal. This time Taryn's love of drama had gotten a sweet man killed and Lacey wasn't about to hold back for the sake of keeping the peace.

"Well then, give me your half of the air-conditioning and I'll be out of your hair," Taryn said haughtily. "The workman won't come back until it's paid."

"Taryn!" Lacey snapped. "I don't have time for you and your bloody air-conditioning unit nonsense."

She sounded just like Gina. The word "bloody" had slipped out naturally.

"I just heard you shell out five hundred for a ring," Taryn said. "So you can definitely afford it."

The nerve of the woman! She should count herself lucky that Lacey hadn't sued her for bashing a hole in their wall without her consent in the first place!

"Just GET OUT!" Lacey yelled.

Taryn narrowed her eyes. "It's always great to catch up with you, Lacey."

Having gotten in the last final cutting sarcastic remark, Taryn spun on her spindly heel and left.

Lacey's anger didn't subside, even if she had gotten a small victory over Taryn for once.

"Come on, Chester," she said. "Let's go see Tom."

She needed someone to vent to. There were no customers coming into the store at the moment, so it wouldn't exactly hurt sales for her to lock up in the middle of the day.

She locked the French doors securely to make sure no more evil boutique owners decided to march in unannounced, and left out the front, locking the door behind her.

She crossed the cobblestones with Chester, still brimming with the irritation Taryn had provoked in her, and entered Tom's patisserie.

The gingerbread castle was complete and took up one of the tables. It looked marvelous. It would be even more impressive once Tom had worked out how to set up the projector and beam a little ghost girl inside.

"Hello, Lacey," Emmanuel said from the counter.

"Is he in the back?" Lacey asked, barely slowing down her march.

"Of course," Emmanuel replied with a smile.

Lacey forced out a smile and headed into the kitchen.

This time, Tom was surrounded by pumpkins.

"Now what's going on?" she asked.

He glanced over his shoulder.

"Lacey?" he said, with a grin. He looked back at the pumpkins. "This? I'm catering for a sweet sixteen and the birthday girl is a grain-free vegan. So I'm trying to perfect a pumpkin and carrot birthday cake."

"I don't even know what grain-free entails," Lacey muttered.

"It means no flour," Tom said. "And no flour replacement. And obviously no egg, because she's a vegan."

"That sounds… tricky," Lacey said.

"Tricky but not impossible," he said with a grin.

Lacey just couldn't do it, the whole small talk thing. She was in too much of a mood. Her only lead had gone cold, and then Taryn had infuriated her.

She rested her backside on the counter and launched into her rant.

"My best lead just went cold," she said.

"Finnbar?" Tom asked.

"No, the Jeep Cherokee driver. You remember, the one who elbowed me when we were at Chumley's?"

Tom flashed her a disapproving expression. "What happened to keeping me in the loop?"

Lacey tensed. She'd promised Tom she'd tell him about her investigation, and had totally failed to. Why? Because she was still holding onto the situation back in Rye with her father? Because she still quietly—and unfairly—blamed him for her father disappearing again?

"Lacey?" Tom asked again. "Well? What did you do?"

"Nothing," Lacey replied, holding her hands up. "I just arranged an appointment with him, to value the ring he was trying to shill when we were at Chumley's."

Tom's eyes narrowed. "You set a trap," he translated. "To lure him to your store."

"Yes," Lacey admitted.

Tom looked thoroughly displeased. His eyes, which were usually such a beautiful sparkly green, became dull with defeat.

"You told me you'd be careful," he said, sadly.

"I am being careful," Lacey assured him. "He wasn't the culprit. So no harm done."

Tom just shook his head. "What made you think he was the best lead in the first place?"

"He saw me buy the tomato painting. Other than us, he's the only other person who knew about the Carson Desi."

Tom paused, his expression turning thoughtful. "Are you sure about that?"

"About what?"

"About who knew the painting was there. You know the usual culprits are the ones with a personal relationship. Crimes of passion and all that."

"Edwin didn't have anyone close to him," Lacey explained. "His wife was dead. He had no kids. No grandkids."

"What about friends?" Tom asked. "Associates? I mean, did you ever stop to wonder where Edwin got the Carson Desi painting in the first place? Why he felt the need to hide it? Why he sold it to an innocent party without them knowing? He must've had some contacts in the art world to even end up with it in his possession. Maybe a shady one."

Lacey wasn't convinced. "I really don't think he knew the Desi was hidden behind the tomato painting when he sold it to me."

"Why not?" Tom pressed. "What if Edwin wasn't this sweet old innocent man like you assumed he was? You know looks can be deceiving."

Lacey didn't like the way Tom was talking about Edwin, with suspicion, like he might've deserved what had happened to him.

She folded her arms and raised an eyebrow.

"What do you mean by that?" she challenged.

Tom met her with a steady gaze. "Brooke," he said, simply.

Lacey felt the word like a punch in the gut. Brooke, the Australian coffee-shop owner, had been becoming a fast friend of Lacey's until Lacey had discovered she'd killed a local man. Then she'd turned on Lacey, threatening her with a knife. Lacey had been lucky to escape with her life. She'd had a hard time putting it behind her.

"Why would you bring up Brooke?" she asked, feeling hurt.

"Because," Tom said, "you never would've known from looking at her what she'd been through, or the secrets she was keeping. All I'm saying is consider the idea that Edwin knew all about the Carson Desi all along. That there was a reason he was hiding it. That there was someone specifically he was hiding it from..."

Crime of passion, Lacey thought.

She realized what her next step was. She was going to research Edwin.

CHAPTER TWENTY TWO

Lacey knew Edwin wasn't the sort of man to have left behind a digital footprint. He was far too old to have even bothered with the internet and all the fuss that came with it. If there were any traces of him or his store for Lacey to find at all, they would be in physical print form. And the only place to access those was the library.

Lacey walked to Wilfordshire's recently built library-cum-theater space. It was in a beautiful square glass building, the design somehow have been approved by the pedantic council and fussy townspeople. It was becoming something of a nice tourist spot, situated on a newly pedestrianized road off the main high street with a square and fountain and trees to offer shade. With a vintage ice cream van and coffee stall permanently set up there along with picnic tables, the newly designed area was becoming something of a tourist hotspot. Having a bit of art and culture in the town was a great lure as well, and mixing the privately owned theater with the publicly owned library meant it was more likely to weather any future financial storms. Because if there was one thing Lacey had learned as a business owner, it was that one was never far from a financial storm.

The weather was warm, though slightly cooler than it had been over the last few days. If Lacey hadn't been on her way to research a murdered man, she might have enjoyed the tranquility of it all. But instead, she was tense, and felt tightly wound.

She headed inside the library's main atrium, which was perfectly air conditioned, and went up to the reception desk. A studious-looking young woman who reminded Lacey of herself from her youth was manning the counter. She glanced up as Lacey approached and smiled.

"How can I help you today?" she asked, shoving her mousy brown hair behind her ear.

"Do you guys keep newspaper records and that sort of thing?" Lacey asked.

"Local newspapers, yes," the girl told her. "We have every *Wilfordshire Weekly* going back to its first print after the war."

"That's great," Lacey said, before realizing copies of the *Wilfordshire Weekly* wouldn't be much use at all. Chumley's was located in Exeter. "What about other local regions? Exeter and the surrounding area?"

"You'll want to check the digitized records," the young librarian told her. "All the libraries in the UK are synced up. As long as they've gotten around to scanning it, it'll be on there."

"Thanks," Lacey said.

She headed off to the research area where the library computers were located. She took a seat between two guys in their twenties who gave off college-student vibes. The closest university, in Exeter, was beginning to accept students for the new academic year, Lacey noted. She'd be seeing groups of college day trippers coming to Wilfordshire soon enough.

She logged onto the library's archive system and typed in the name *Edwin Cross.* The first thing to pop up, unsurprisingly, was an obituary.

Lacey felt her throat tighten with emotion as she clicked the link and began to read.

The obituary had been submitted by Edwin's brother-in-law, Bryan Vallins, and confirmed what Lacey already knew. He had no children, no grandchildren, and was *"Finally reunited in Heaven with his beloved wife, Diane."*

It was a touching message, one befitting the man Lacey thought Edwin to be.

She closed the obituary and added some more key words. *Antiques. Chumley's.*

It didn't take long for her to find a newspaper article. The scanned copy was grainy and slightly difficult to read. She squinted.

"Exeter Man Wins Antique Award.

"Antiques dealer Edwin Cross, 35, has won the industry's top award after being named Antiques Dealer of the Year in the annual British Antiques and Collectables Awards. Mr. Cross started selling bric-a-brac at 15, with a Saturday stall in Exeter market. By 20, he'd made the switch to antiques and was the proud owner of a thriving store on Queen's Street."

Interesting. So Edwin owned a different store before Chumley's, one located on Queen's Street, a prime location beside one of Exeter's train stations. Lacey wondered why he'd chosen to move to such a rundown converted barn on the outskirts of town, when it seemed his city-located store was a success.

She continued reading.

"Mr. Cross credits his success to honest pricing and keeping up with the trends.

"'I'm a young man, myself,' he stated. 'I know what people my age like. If I pick up a dining table for fifty pounds and sell it on for fifty five, I know I've done an honest day's work.'"

Lacey couldn't help but smile at the words of the dear old man. Even in his youth he hadn't been greedy.

She scrolled down to the accompanying photograph. It showed a young Edwin standing proudly behind the counter of his store. Unfortunately, his face was distorted by a badly placed fold in the paper. But what hadn't been obscured was the painting hanging right behind his till.

It was the tomato painting. The very painting behind which Lacey had found the Carson Desi.

Lacey's heart started pounding. It was peculiar. A coincidence at the least. At the most, a clue.

She thought it through. Not only had Edwin been in possession of the tomato painting for so many years, at least since he was in his thirties, but he'd once liked it enough to use it as decoration. So why had he sold it to her? Was Tom's hunch right? Had Edwin known about the masterpiece hidden behind it all along? Had he been hiding it from someone? Someone who'd recently traced the painting to him? Someone who he was so afraid of he'd decided to get rid of the painting by putting it on sale?

Lacey sat back in the seat, her mind going a mile a minute.

She decided to change course and research the elusive Carson Desi instead. All she knew about him was what Finnbar had told her the evening they'd discovered the painting. Maybe there was something in his past that might give her a clue as to why Edwin had hidden the painting all those years.

She went online and began to research.

It didn't take long for her to realize Finnbar hadn't exaggerated a thing. Carson Desi really had never made a public appearance. No one even knew what he looked like, though most fans seemed to agree from his Indonesian surname he'd be brown-skinned and dark-eyed.

And Finnbar was also right that his reclusiveness added to the mystique. Carson Desi had accumulated quite a passionate fanbase.

When he suddenly stopped producing paintings in the eighties, those very same hardcore fans bombarded the police with requests for welfare checks. Some even tried to get a petition into parliament demanding the police open a missing person's case! After so much pressure the police were forced to issue a statement explaining, "The artist known as Carson Desi is safe and well and not a missing person. We will issue no other statements on this case." Their short and dismissive statement had obviously done nothing to put the issue to rest, and conspiracy theories abounded.

Lacey even found a whole website devoted to the mystery of Carson Desi, which had over a thousand subscribers and had been updated as recently as last month! The forum was full of theories, the most popular and active being, *"Carson Desi Was Murdered,"* *"Carson Desi WAS Lucian Freud: Evidence Megathread,"* and *"Carson Desi was a communist spy killed by MI5."* Among the lesser commented ones were, *"Proof Aliens Abducted Carson Desi"* and *"Carson Desi's Links to the Illuminati."*

She found one of the least sensationalist threads and clicked on it.

"Carson Desi was born in Indonesia during the Japanese occupation of WWII. During peacetime, and as an infant, he emigrated to Britain with his mother, where he was home-educated. His loose education allowed him the freedom to explore his creative and artistic talents, and he began producing artworks at a very young age."

The post went on and on, and Lacey scrolled down to see the comments that had been left beneath it.

"NONE of that is fact!" a rather heated-up forum member had posted. *"Stop pretending you know more than any of us! The TRUTH is, other than his close friends and family, NO ONE KNOWS!"*

The original poster had then replied with, *"All this can be seen in Carson's artwork. He left many clues for fans to piece together, assuming they're intelligent enough to do so."*

The rest of the thread descended into an argument, and Lacey stopped reading.

"Hold on..." Lacey suddenly said aloud.

The men in the booths either side of her turned and frowned.

"Sorry," she whispered.

Quickly, she pulled up the newspaper clipping of Edwin in his Queen's Street store, his first store before he'd moved to Chumley's. It didn't take long for her to discover that Edwin had relocated from there to the obscure shack in the 1980s. Almost as if… he'd wanted to disappear.

Suddenly, Lacey's mind started running on overdrive. Before she could stop herself, she was on her feet, crying out, "Edwin was Carson Desi!"

A chorus of *"shhh"* greeted her loud exclamation.

Lacey felt her cheeks burn.

She sank back into her seat, trying to make herself as small as possible, as her mind raced through the new theory.

It all fit. If Edwin himself was Carson Desi, that would explain why he had relocated his business. It explained why he hadn't wanted to take the painting back from her—because the model was someone he knew personally, an ex-lover maybe. Someone, perhaps, who he'd kept a personal portrait of, but who'd broken his heart in the eighties, prompting him to quit painting and disappear into obscurity.

Lacey scanned the forums again, rereading a particularly pertinent comment.

"The TRUTH is, other than his close friends and family, NO ONE KNOWS."

If she wanted to find out whether Edwin was Carson Desi, there was only one person in his close family she knew was still alive to ask. His brother-in-law, Bryan Vallins, the one who'd posted the obituary.

But he was in Exeter and Lacey wasn't allowed to leave town.

Unless she did it carefully? If a famous artist could keep his identity hidden for decades and disappear without a trace, surely Lacey could sneak out of Wilfordshire without being spotted…

She hurried out of the library, a plan of action formulating in her mind.

CHAPTER TWENTY THREE

Of all the silly things Lacey had done in her life, this really was one of the silliest. She was impersonating Gina, just to get out of town.

She knew her champagne-colored Volvo was far too recognizable, so she'd asked Gina to borrow hers. And since Gina herself was rather recognizable, she'd also dressed herself up in a pair of bright-framed sunglasses and wrapped her head in a gray scarf to make it look like hair. As long as no one tried to flag her down for a chat, she should be able to get out of town, unimpeded, in her Gina disguise.

In the back seat sat the original painting of tomatoes she had bought from Edwin in the first place. Just in case the picture, or the frame that had been concealing the Carson Desi, helped jog any memories in Edwin's brother-in-law.

Nerves crackled through her as Lacey reached the intersection leading out of Wilfordshire. She checked for traffic and, seeing nothing, pulled onto the road that headed out of town.

So far so good, she thought with relief.

Lacey's SATNAV directed her toward Edwin's brother-in-law's home. It turned out he didn't live that far away from where Chumley's store was located, in the small town of Widecombe on the outskirts of Exeter. It was a beautiful little place, filled with churches and spires and dinky cafés down narrow, winding roads. Lacey guessed from the architecture and the period it heralded from that the town had grown up around a pit stop for travelers, the sort of place that had originally contained inns, taverns, stables to rest the horses in, and barns for storing goods.

Lacey took a left turn onto the residential street of her final destination, and slowed to a halt outside a cottage.

"You have reached your destination," her SATNAV told her.

Lacey killed the engine and peered through the window at the cottage. It was cute and humble, just like she imagined Edwin's home would look.

She checked her rearview mirror in case she'd been spotted by the cops and followed here, but saw no one. She was relieved to have successfully gotten out of Wilfordshire without being seen.

Deciding it was safe to exit the car, Lacey reached for the door handle. Chester barked and she paused. It was only then Lacey realized she was still wearing the scarf wrapped around her head and the pair of brightly colored sunglasses.

"Thanks, Chester," she told him, quickly removing her disguise. "That could've been very embarrassing!"

Lacey got out of the car, dog in tow, and they headed up the garden path of Edwin's brother-in-law's house. Lacey felt a mixture of nerves and excitement as she knocked. Was she about to find the information she needed to crack the case? She certainly felt closer now than she had before. But she still felt nervous about intruding on this grieving man's life.

She took a breath and knocked.

A short moment passed before the door was answered by an old man in a knitted brown cardigan. He was very tall, at least six feet, though Lacey guessed him closer to six-three or even -four. He had a crooked nose, with a bump at the bridge that looked genetic rather than acquired from a break.

He scanned Lacey and Chester with curious gray eyes.

"Hello?" he said. He had the same friendly Yorkshire accent as Edwin, and hearing it caused a pang of grief to swell in Lacey's chest.

"Are you Bryan Vallins?" she asked, keeping the quiver out of her voice.

"Aye," he said with a nod. "Can I help you?"

"I'm sorry to bother you," Lacey said. "I'm here about Edwin."

At the mention of his deceased brother-in-law, Bryan's face fell. The laugh lines that had been so pronounced before completely disappeared. In their place came frown lines and a downturn at the corners of his mouth.

"Oh," he said, with a distinctly morose tone. "What about him?"

"I knew him through work," Lacey said, as gently as she could.

She'd already been feeling intrusive. Now that she'd upset the man she felt guilty.

"I'm in antiques," she explained. "I shopped at Chumley's. I'd like to think I was becoming a friend of Edwin's before he died."

"That's nice," Bryan replied, in a stilted manner. "He didn't have many people in his life."

Just then, a female voice from a distance behind him called out. "Bryan? Bryan, who is it? Who's there?"

She, too, had the same strong Yorkshire accent as Edwin and Bryan.

"It's friend of Edwin's," he called back over his shoulder.

"Well, don't leave them standing on the doorstep!" the woman said. "Invite them in. I'll make a pot of tea."

Bryan looked back at Lacey, his bushy gray eyebrows raised into a question. "Want to come in?"

He took a step back from the door, but Lacey shook her head.

"Thank you, but no," she said. "I wasn't planning on stopping long. I just have a few questions."

"My wife will already have put the kettle on," he said, smiling with endearment for the woman Lacey could hear clattering about in the kitchen. "So you may as well. She loves guests. Especially four-legged furry ones." He looked down at Chester. "That's a handsome fellow you've got there."

Chester barked happily and wagged his tail with pride. Lacey decided if Bryan passed Chester's test, then he must be safe enough.

"I guess one cuppa won't hurt," she said.

She stepped inside and followed Bryan along a corridor decorated with floral wallpaper, and lit by wall sconces in the shape of tulips. She entered after him into the living room, which was small but beautifully maintained, with a comfy-looking brown couch and matching armchair facing a large TV in the corner, beside a lace-covered window. There was a fireplace with a black iron grate inside and brown tiles surrounding it. Above the wooden mantelpiece hung several paintings and a large, vintage map of Yorkshire.

"You're all from Yorkshire?" Lacey asked.

"Leeds," Bryan said with a nod. "Edwin was my best friend ever since nursery school. Then he married my sister, and became my brother."

It was a touching story, and Lacey felt a pang of sadness for the man who was no longer here with them. They were clearly very close if they'd known each other for almost the entirety of their lives.

Lacey's eyes roved from the map to the artworks beside it. There were some very interesting pieces—bright, bold abstracts and surrealist portraits. Even a couple of nudes. It wasn't really the sort of thing Lacey would expect to see in the home of an old couple. There wasn't a single oil landscape in sight. Bryan and his wife clearly had an interesting taste in art.

111

Lacey was about to ask about the collection when Bryan's wife entered the room holding a tray, teapot, and mugs. She was the opposite of her husband in appearance—short where he was tall, tubby where he was lanky. The pair reminded Lacey of the couple in old nursery rhyme, Jack Spratt.

The woman took one look at Chester and squealed.

"Dog!" she cried, almost dropping the tray in her delight.

Chester, who loved nothing more than showing off just how much of a good boy he truly was, ran up to her and started nuzzling into her legs.

"Oh, what a gorgeous boy you are, what a gorgeous boy," she exclaimed, discarding the tray hastily on the dining table and crouching down to fuss over Chester.

Bryan darted over and grabbed the tray, which was sticking precariously over the edge of the table. He flashed Lacey a red-faced smile, as if to say, *Told you she liked dogs.*

Bryan coughed and his wife glanced up.

"We have guests," he said, gesturing with his head to Lacey.

"Sorry," the woman exclaimed, as she straightened up. "I'm Joy. You're a friend of Edwin's, is that right?"

She held her hand out and Lacey shook it. She was a plump woman with jolly cheeks and the energetic exuberance of a primary school teacher.

"That's right," Lacey said. "I work in antiques as well. That's how we met. I'm sorry for your loss."

"Thank you," Joy said, earnestly. "And I'm sorry for yours, too."

Lacey felt a little disingenuous accepting their sympathy. She'd barely known Edwin, after all, and she was only here on a fact-finding mission. But even in that short amount of time, she had felt a connection to him. If he'd lived, she was sure he would've become a dear work associate, akin to Percy Jackson.

"Shall we sit?" Joy said, gesturing to the couch.

Lacey sank into the soft fabric couch beside Bryan. Joy took the armchair. Bryan poured the tea and handed a mug to Lacey.

"I guess you're wondering why I'm here," Lacey said, wrapping both hands around the mug. "I had a question. About Edwin."

"Go on," Bryan prompted.

"I bought a painting from his antiques store and found another hidden behind it. A very expensive one."

Joy leaned over and gave her husband's knee a playful smack. "That sounds like Edwin all over, doesn't it? He always did silly things like that, didn't he?"

Bryan nodded, and Joy continued.

"Back when we lived in Leeds, Edwin would set up an Easter egg hunt every year. They got more and more elaborate over the years. Honestly, those blasted things could last. Do you remember, Bry?" She started to chuckle. "Oh, he certainly loved to surprise people. Puzzles. Treasure hunts. He loved things like that."

Interesting, Lacey thought.

"The thing is," Lacey said, tightening her hands around the mug with nervous anticipation. "The painting was by Carson Desi."

The atmosphere in the room changed instantly. Joy, who'd been so chatty before, suddenly clammed up. Bryan, who'd been the quieter of the two, happy to take a backseat while his wife took the lead, sat up straighter as if to take control.

"How very fortunate for you," he mumbled. "I guess you hit the jackpot."

Lacey watched the pair carefully. They'd become more stilted. More awkward.

"Do you know why Edwin would be so generous?" Lacey queried.

Husband and wife exchanged blank looks.

"That's just the way he was," Joy said. "A kind man. Giving. Caring."

Lacey nodded, but it didn't seem like an adequate enough explanation to her. Not even the kindest man in the world would simply give away millions of pounds.

"But the painting is worth millions," Lacey pressed. "That goes above and beyond caring."

They exchanged another look.

"Well, y—yes, I suppose it does," Joy stammered.

Whatever they knew about Edwin, they weren't about to share it with Lacey.

"Did Edwin paint?" she asked, changing course.

"He tried," Joy said. "Though he wasn't particularly good at it."

"So it was a hobby for him. Not a career."

"Definitely a hobby," Joy said, nodding with the sort of overexaggeration someone might when they were lying.

"Edwin was no Carson Desi," Bryan said. "I should know. I'm an art dealer. Or I was before I retired."

113

He pointed to the array of striking artworks Lacey had been wondering about earlier. That explained his eclectic taste in art, at least.

Lacey scanned the artworks, taking a moment to ponder Bryan's words. She found it particularly interesting that Bryan had made the link without her asking. Either he'd read between the lines and worked out Lacey suspected Edwin Cross and Carson Desi were one and the same person, or he'd accidentally let slip the secret he was trying to keep hidden.

She retrieved the tomato painting and showed it to them. "Is this one of Edwin's?"

"Oh yes!" Joy exclaimed. "It's that blasted tomato painting." She started laughing. "We used to tease him about it because of how awful it was. Do you remember, Bryan?"

"I remember," her husband replied with a smirk. "He hung it up in his store just to prove a point."

"That was just his sense of humor," Joy added.

Lacey was stunned. So the tomatoes were painted by Edwin. And if he was the original artist, then he surely must've been the person who framed the painting? So he definitely knew the Carson Desi was hidden behind it.

Lacey's suspicion that he was the artist became even stronger.

He'd made it clear he didn't want money, or the hassle that came with it. He must've decided it was safe now to sell his hidden masterpiece because he was reaching the final years of his life. He probably wasn't expecting Lacey to immediately discover the secret masterpiece he'd hidden behind it, then come back to her store with all her probing, nosy questions. If Edwin was indeed the reclusive Carson Desi, then didn't it all make perfect sense? His reclusiveness was all part of his silly sense of humor. He'd cheekily hidden his masterpiece behind a deliberately terrible tomato painting just to amuse himself, knowing when it was one day discovered, it would become a funny footnote to the mysterious life of Carson Desi.

Lacey's pulse started racing with excitement.

"This tomato painting was in front of the Carson Desi," she explained. "I think Edwin used the tomato painting to hide his masterpiece."

Bryan immediately snapped his lips shut, as if he'd realized he'd said too much. Or maybe Lacey was reading into it?

She continued, laying her theory on the table to see how the couple reacted.

"I think Edwin was the artist. He was the one who framed the silly tomato painting, and he hid his masterpiece behind it."

The couple looked skeptical.

"But dear, look at the quality," Bryan said. "Why would anyone choose to display that awful tomato painting instead of their genuinely good painting?"

"Because that's the joke," Lacey said. "You said yourself he hung the painting because you teased him about it. What if he was quietly getting the last laugh, by knowing a masterpiece was hidden just behind it?"

Bryan shook his head. "The tomato was clearly done by an amateur. You can tell just by looking at the brush strokes. Carson Desi was a rare genius of our time. The sort of artist who will be remembered for centuries to come."

"Which you both know Edwin would have hated," Lacey said. "Edwin was an understated man. A simple guy. He didn't want hassle or attention. He didn't even care about making money."

"Or maybe he just isn't who you think he is," Bryan said. "The most simple explanation is usually the right one. Edwin needed a frame so he could hang his tomato painting and goad us with it. The Carson Desi painting just happened to be the right size for his needs. I'm sure he had no idea he was covering up a masterwork."

Joy clapped. "There we go. Mystery solved."

But Lacey wasn't buying it. And she wasn't done questioning the couple. They knew more than they were letting on. It was obvious in their micro-expressions, in their gestures. Lacey was far too perceptive to fall for their act.

"How would he have gotten hold of the masterwork in the first place?" she challenged.

Just then, her attention was drawn to something on the mantelpiece. Like most people, the couple had put family portraits on the mantel, and there were some from many years ago. Lacey recognized both Joy and Bryan standing on the beach in their modest bathing suits along with a much younger version of Edwin. There was also a woman, presumably Edwin's wife, and she looked strikingly familiar.

Lacey gasped.

She was the woman in the painting!

"I knew it!" Lacey cried, jumping up from the couch. She grasped the photograph in both hands. "Edwin was Carson Desi!" She spun the photograph around and tapped the woman standing beside Edwin. "The painting I found was of his wife!"

Both husband and wife looked incredibly uncomfortable, avoiding making eye contact with Lacey.

"You were both in on the secret," Lacey continued, as it all started coming together in her mind.

She pointed at Bryan.

"Were you his dealer?" she asked. "Is that how he was able to keep his identity secret for so long? Because he kept it in the family?"

But before Bryan had a chance to answer her barrage of questions, Lacey's phone started ringing.

"Hold on," she said, grabbing it and heading into the corridor for privacy.

If that was her mom again, she'd lose it. But it wasn't. It was Tom.

Lacey answered the call. "Tom? What is it? I'm right in the middle of something."

"The police are at your shop," Tom said.

"What? Why?"

"I think you'd better get back here."

CHAPTER TWENTY FOUR

Lacey's mind raced. Had someone seen through her Gina disguise and tipped the police off about her leaving town? If the police knew she'd spent the day in Widecombe, could they arrest her?

She ended her call with Tom and rushed back into Bryan and Joy's living room.

The couple were sitting exactly where she'd left them, but the atmosphere in the room had grown considerably more tense during her absence. Lacey got the distinct impression they'd shared a whispered heated debate while she'd been otherwise occupied, presumably regarding Lacey's discovery of the photograph proving that Edwin's late wife was the model in the painting. Lacey wanted nothing more than to stay here and eke the truth out of them. Because they clearly knew more than they were letting on, and she was clearly very close to getting them to spill the beans. If they were at odds over telling her about it, she was probably close to breaking them. But she didn't have a choice. She had to get back to her store.

"I'm sorry, but I have to leave," she told the couple.

"But you've not finished your tea," Joy commented.

"Let the woman leave if she wants to," Bryan said in a warning tone.

So Joy was the one who wanted to spill, Lacey theorized. Once she was done attending to whatever situation was taking place back home, perhaps she could call them and speak to the wife.

She clicked her fingers and Chester came trotting over to her.

"Don't worry," she told them, from the living room doorway. "I won't tell anyone about who Edwin really was. Thanks for the tea."

And with that she whirled out of their house, leaving the two looking like their whole world had just been turned upside down.

*

It was dark by the time Lacey reached Wilfordshire. Her nerves were all over the place. She'd spent the entire drive going over every scenario that might have caused the police to be at her store, each one more terrible than the last.

She turned Gina's car onto the high street and immediately saw flashing lights coming from the end of the street where her store was situated. This wasn't just about her skipping town. Something bad had happened. Something really bad.

She hit the gas and sped along the bumpy cobblestones. Then she parked wonkily, one wheel on the curbside.

Tom was standing by her store entrance talking to several officers. Blue lights flashed all over him.

Lacey threw open the driver's door and ran toward him. Chester hurried after her.

"Lacey?" Tom said, looking surprised to see her suddenly standing there. His eyes went over her shoulder and he frowned. "Were you driving Gina's car?"

"It's a long story," she said, dismissively. "What happened?"

Before Tom could answer, one of the officers stepped forward. He had slicked back black hair that reminded Lacey of a 1940s businessman.

"Are you the store's proprietor?" he asked.

"Yes," Lacey said. "What is it? What's happened?"

"I'm afraid your store has been ransacked."

Lacey gasped. "Someone broke in?"

The officer shook his head. "There was no sign of forced entry. Either the back door was left unlocked, or the person who did this had a key." He took out his notebook. "Can you tell me who has a key to the premises?"

"It's just me and Gina," Lacey said, automatically. Then she paused, and a feeling of trepidation overcame her. "And Finnbar."

As the officer wrote down their names, Tom flashed Lacey a questioning look. He knew she'd once considered Finnbar her prime suspect. He didn't even have to ask her aloud to know Finnbar had made his way straight back onto the suspect list, right at the top, underlined in red.

"I saw a shadow through the window," Tom told her. "I ran over and scared them off. I didn't see who it was."

Lacey went inside her store. She and Gina had only just finished straightening it up and now it was in more of a state of disarray than before. She gasped at the damaged pieces all over the place.

"Your insurance will cover this, won't it?" Tom asked.

Lacey nodded, hypnotically. "Sure. But that's not the point. Some of these pieces are one of a kind. They've survived for centuries, and now they're worthless."

Her heart broke for all the history that had been wiped out in the blink of an eye.

"Can you tell us everything that's been stolen?" the officer asked.

"Sure," Lacey said.

She began tiptoeing her way through the detritus. "Wait. I don't think anything's been stolen at all."

"How curious," came the distinctive voice of Superintendent Turner.

Lacey swirled. He was standing in the doorway, framed by the moonlight. He took a step inside, glass crunching under his foot.

"Where were you this evening?" he asked.

"Visiting a friend," Lacey said, not mentioning that her so-called "friend" lived in a different town.

"That's interesting," he replied. "Because your car has been parked in the same spot all day."

He'd been watching her.

"I borrowed Gina's," Lacey said. "My air conditioner is broken."

She needed to stop lying. That's how the cops caught people out, by getting them to make up more and more lies until they couldn't keep up with themselves anymore.

"How unfortunate," Superintendent Turner added.

He took another step closer, the glass crunching. Chester began to growl.

"Hello, Fido," the detective said.

"Chester, heel," Lacey warned.

Her dog backed down.

Lacey looked at the detective and folded her arms.

"Are you here about my store being ransacked?" she asked. "Or did you just fancy popping by to talk about my car?"

"I'm actually investigating a very similar crime that happened earlier in the day," Turner said. "There are enough similarities between that crime and this one to suppose they may be linked."

"Oh?" Lacey asked.

Superintendent Turner nodded. "Yes. There was a ransacking at a little place known as … Chumley's."

Lacey gasped. "Someone broke into Edwin's store too?"

It couldn't be a coincidence. Whoever had broken into Lacey's store and Edwin's store was surely the same person.

And Lacey thought she knew just what had happened.

The killer didn't have the painting.

They went to Chumley's to steal it, but had murdered Edwin instead, possibly because he interrupted them mid-theft. They'd left emptyhanded. Edwin must've hidden the Carson Desi painting. Hidden it so well even the cops hadn't found it during their search. She'd told them to look behind other paintings, and Superintendent Turner had made it sound like he'd done just that. Now she wondered if he'd been bluffing.

Whoever killed Edwin was still searching for the painting.

And by the state of her ransacked store, they thought she might still have it.

Would she be killed next?

CHAPTER TWENTY FIVE

Lacey sat crossed-legged on the floor of her store, dustpan and brush in hand, and pushed back a dark curl from her face. She'd been growing her hair out all year (ever since Taryn had copied her asymmetrical bobbed hairstyle) and it was getting long enough now to become an encumbrance, especially during the grueling tidying up of her store the ransacking had forced her to undertake. Maybe it was time to give up any pretense of fashion and just invest in some colorful scrunchies like Gina.

The brief moment of humor disappeared as Lacey began to sweep up the shattered remains of a set of crystal sherry glasses. She remembered buying the six-piece set on one of her first ever stock trips to London with Gina, when everything had felt new and exciting. She'd been looking forward to selling them on to a new customer. Having that moment taken away from her stung. Having her store damaged felt as painful to Lacey as if the broken glass had slashed her.

The glass shards tinkled musically as Lacey swept them into the dustpan. Tears pricked her eyes.

All that history, gone in an instant, she thought, mournfully.

She glanced about her. There was still so much to do to get the store back to normal. Too much, in fact. Lacey felt overwhelmed just thinking about it all. The last thing she needed right now was another huge task to bear the burden of. Her mom and sister were constantly hassling her about wedding preparations, the letter she'd sent to her father remained unanswered, and now all her mental energy was being taken up by her investigation into Edwin's murder.

Even as she swept, her mind fixated on the investigation. She was at a complete dead end. She had no idea who the killer might be. She didn't even have any leads left to pursue. Something was missing. Like the shards of the sherry glass in her dustpan, there were too many missing pieces to put it all together. She had to find the missing pieces. Ones that would pull all the threads together.

Just then, her phone dinged with an incoming message. From his basket in the corner, Chester let out a single, grumpy *yip*. Even while half-asleep he still took his secondary alarm duties very seriously.

Expecting to see a message from her mom or Naomi, Lacey peered over at her cell. Instead, the message had come from her ex-husband, David.

Can you give me a call at some point, please? it said simply.

Lacey hadn't returned any of his telephone calls. Or listened to any of his voicemails. Contact with David never brought anything good, and right now the last thing she wanted to do was invite more negativity into her life.

On second thought...

Lacey put down her dustpan and brush. It wasn't like she could get that much lower. Edwin's murder and her store's ransacking had put everything sharply into perspective. What could her ex-husband really say to bring her down more than she already was? Whatever petty jibe he was going to throw at her, she didn't have to give it any power. She would just let it wash over her. David was in her past. He didn't matter anymore. What mattered was solving Edwin's murder and protecting her livelihood.

She may as well just bite the bullet. The longer she left it lingering, the more irritating it became, and the more she allowed it to matter.

She stood, abandoning the sweeping task, and went over to the red velvet love seat. As she sank into it, she swallowed her pride and dialed David.

"Lacey!" he exclaimed when the call was answered.

He sounded jovial, like he was smiling. Lacey narrowed her eyes suspiciously. David didn't usually sound happy when he was speaking to her. She couldn't help but wonder where this was going.

"You asked me to call," Lacey said, cautiously.

"I did," he replied, in that same happy tone. "I've been trying to get hold of you to say congratulations on your engagement."

Lacey was astonished. Had David really just *congratulated* her? The same man who'd sulked when she'd been promoted because it meant she'd have the higher salary?

"Um... thanks?" she replied, sounding wholly unconvinced.

"I'm really glad you've found someone," David continued.

This was just getting stranger and stranger. Their divorce had been acrimonious. David had behaved like a petty child, demanding she change her name back to her maiden name on every single piece of ID she owned, right down to her library card and gym membership, demanding alimony payments from her, and proposing to the first fertile woman he'd found within a five-mile radius. Lacey struggled to believe anything he was saying was genuine.

"You are?" she challenged.

On the other of the line, David started to chuckle.

"Of course I am!" he exclaimed. "I never wanted you to be alone, Lacey. Or to suffer. I moved on quickly because I had a very clear vision for my future and just had to find someone who shared it with me. I was worried that you might struggle to find someone because you were never sure of anything."

At first, Lacey heard it as a back-handed compliment. The sort she'd get from Taryn. But as David's words sank in, Lacey realized that even if he'd intended it as criticism, she didn't need to perceive it that way. Because, really, it was the plain and simple truth.

Their marriage had ended over one very clear, non-negotiable difference in opinion: having children. David wanted them immediately, and Lacey wasn't sure when, or if, she ever would. His vision was clear. Hers was not. He wasn't backing down, and she wasn't going to be forced.

Divorce was the only solution to their problem. And didn't it all work out for the best for everyone in the end? David's new fiancée was due to give birth in the coming months, and Lacey had everything she'd never even realized she wanted. (Aside, of course, from her father being back in her life.) But beyond that—Tom, Crag Cottage, the store, Chester, Gina, Wilfordshire—all of that had come to her because of her divorce. She hadn't had a clear vision for her future back then because she hadn't even known where to begin untangling her own desires from his. If David hadn't forced her hand, maybe she never would.

"I appreciate that," Lacey said earnestly. "And I know what I want now."

She thought of Tom, his slightly straggly chestnut brown hair streaked with sun-bleached strands, his playful approach to life, his megawatt smile, his twinkling green eyes. All that stuff she'd been stressing about over Tom and Norah meant nothing. They had the rest of their lives to get to know the fine details.

"I'm glad," David continued. "And now that we're both moving on with our lives, I figured we should drop the whole alimony stuff."

Now Lacey really was astounded. It had been a bitter moment in their divorce proceedings when David had somehow managed to wrangle alimony payments from her.

"I think it would be best, don't you?" her ex continued. "So we can start these next chapters of our lives with a clean slate."

"Well, yes—yes, of course I agree," Lacey replied, flummoxed.

Where had all this maturity suddenly come from?

David chuckled. "It's strange isn't it, to be starting all over again at our age? I guess that's the perk of modern life. We stay healthier for longer, so we get to live a couple of lives if we want to. Remarrying at forty isn't as much of a big deal as it was in the past."

Lacey hadn't thought of it this way. When she'd quit her job and left New York, it had felt reckless. Her family had thought she was having a midlife crisis, or mental breakdown, just as her father had done at the same age. But maybe all along, Lacey was just done with her first life, and ready to start her second one. The woman she was at forty was very different from the one who'd walked down the aisle with David all those years ago, after all.

A sense of calm washed over Lacey.

"I suppose this is goodbye," she said.

They'd never actually said the word *goodbye*. David had shouted something about lawyers before he'd slammed the door on their apartment and marriage, and every subsequent telephone conversation since then had ended with one of them abruptly hanging up the phone on the other, upset and annoyed.

"I guess so," David replied. "Goodbye, Lacey. I'll remember the good times."

"I will too," Lacey replied. "Goodbye, David."

CHAPTER TWENTY SIX

Lacey sank back into the love seat, stunned. She never thought she'd get a resolution to her divorce, and now that she had, she didn't quite know how to readjust to it. Was David really completely out of her life for good? Could she really draw a line under that chapter of her life, and start her new one with Tom afresh?

Lacey didn't know what to think. It would take time to process, and she'd have to wait until the situation with Edwin was resolved before she could truly give it the time it deserved.

As her thoughts switched back to Edwin, Lacey suddenly heard key phrases from her conversation with David repeating in her mind. Only this time they held a different significance. As she replayed David's words over and over, she thought of them not in relation to her and David, but in relation to Edwin and his wife instead.

"Starting all over again at our age..."

"We get to live a couple of lives..."

"Remarrying at forty isn't as much of a big deal as it once was..."

Suddenly, it occurred to Lacey that Edwin had married his wife later in life. When she'd spoken to him at Chumley's, he'd mentioned how he and his wife had been married for thirty years before her death some seven years earlier. Bryan's obituary to Edwin had confirmed their thirty years of marriage, too. But for the mathematics to add up, that meant the pair had only tied the knot when they were in their forties.

"They were one another's second go at life," Lacey said to Chester.

He quirked his head to the side curiously, and let out a whinny.

Lacey leapt from the red velvet love seat, pacing the floor of her store as she went back through her meeting with Bryan and Joy Vallins. The black-and-white photo on the mantelpiece showed Edwin and his wife in their modest swimwear, smiling on the beach beside Joy and Bryan. At the time, Lacey had simply assumed that she was looking at a photo of two young couples. Now she realized that wasn't the case at all.

Edwin and his wife had married later in life. They'd spent their first lives apart, not as a couple, despite having known one another since childhood. At the time the photo was taken, the social makeup of the group was entirely different. The picture was actually all about Bryan. It was Bryan at the center, with Bryan's wife, Bryan's sister, and Bryan's best friend around him. *Bryan* was at the center of the group. *Bryan* was the connection.

Lacey ran to the counter, where her notebook was lying beside the telephone. She turned to a fresh page and started feverishly scribbling notes, working so quickly her hand could hardly keep up with her brain.

From his basket, Chester watched her sudden flurry of activity with curiosity.

Soon, Lacey's notepad was covered in scrawls, as she considered this different version of the group and the four individuals within it, and how much the dynamics must have shifted when they'd reached their forties and Edwin had married his best friend's sister.

"When would that have been?" Lacey said, grabbing her calculator.

She punched in a sum, then gasped as the result appeared on her screen. *1980.*

That was when Edwin hit forty years old. That was when the pair had married. And that was the time that just so happened to coincide with Carson Desi's famous vanishing...

"Chester!" Lacey cried, as the cogs of her mind began to turn on overdrive.

Her dog sat straight up, ears pointed toward the ceiling, his attention locked on her.

"What if I've gotten it all the wrong way around?" Lacey said hurriedly. "What if the reason Edwin quit being Carson Desi was because the woman in the portrait had become his wife? What if it was because he was ready to put his first life behind him in order to start his second quiet, married life devoted to the woman he'd waited years to marry?"

Chester barked.

Lacey looked back down at her notepad again, scanning through everything she'd written.

She took every assumption she'd made, every guess she'd had, and flipped it all on its head.

When Lacey was done, she had a whole new theory about who had killed Edwin and why, and it wasn't one she was particularly happy to have come up with.

In her new theory, Bryan wasn't Edwin's trusted art dealer selling his Carson Desi pieces and maintaining his anonymity. In fact, in her new theory, Bryan had been left in the dark, and had no idea Edwin was Carson Desi at all. When Bryan finally worked out his best friend had kept such a huge secret from him, he'd felt betrayed. And instead of being happy about his old childhood friend marrying his sister, he'd been furious. And instead of choosing to move down south from Yorkshire to be close to them, he'd moved down to follow them, to stalk them, to make their lives miserable. Because he was jealous. Obsessed.

Lacey's mind went a mile a minute as the whole new scenario became clearer and clearer in her mind.

Bryan and Edwin were childhood friends. Edwin started his bric-a-brac business, while Bryan pursued a more lucrative career—art dealing. Yet it was Edwin who'd succeeded. He was the one in the newspaper. He was the one winning awards. He was the one with a flourishing business, falling upwards in life. Bryan grew jealous. And then Edwin committed the ultimate betrayal—he married Bryan's sister. People had fallen out over less. Perhaps it was that point when Edwin revealed his identity to his new wife, who revealed it to her brother, and essentially drove the nail into the coffin of their friendship.

Had Bryan learned about the discovery of the Carson Desi painting after Annabella Josher had exposed Lacey? Had he realized that, after all these years, Edwin still had a painting in his possession, one that would sell for hundreds of thousands and make him rich, if he could just get his hands on it…?

Had Bryan killed Edwin?

CHAPTER TWENTY SEVEN

Just then, the bell over the door jangled, interrupting Lacey from her strategizing.

She looked up. It was Finnbar.

"What are you doing here?" she asked. "You know the store's closed."

She'd called both her employees after the ransacking to tell them the store would be closed for the foreseeable future and to take some time off while she sorted everything out with the insurers.

"I wondered if you wanted any help tidying?" Finnbar said, running a nervous hand through his scraggly brown hair.

As sweet as the offer was, Finnbar was probably the last person Lacey wanted to help with tidying. He was so clumsy, he'd probably do more harm than good.

"It's fine," she said, politely declining. "Thanks for stopping by, but I think it's best for me to sort this mess out myself."

Finnbar gave her one of his polite invisible cap nods, and turned to leave.

But just as he opened the door, Lacey was hit with a sudden thought. Finnbar was clumsy, yes. But he was also super smart. Maybe he could help her in another way? Not with the store, but with her investigation…

"On second thought," she said. "There is *something* you could help me with."

Finnbar paused and turned at the door. "Sure. What?"

"Can you help me trace a phone number?" she asked.

Finnbar raised his brown eyebrows. "Should I be worried about all this tracking you're getting me to do? You're not making me an accessory to crime, are you?"

Lacey shook her head. "I promise I'm not stalking anyone. And I'm not doing anything illegal."

Of course, Superintendent Turner might see things differently; Lacey's amateur sleuthing was the bane of his existence.

Finnbar came around behind the counter and sank his skinny behind onto the stool. He flexed his long, knobby-knuckled fingers over the laptop keys, like a runner stretching before a sprint.

"Tell me everything you know about this person," he said.

Lacey began reeling off all the facts she'd acquired about Edwin's brother-in-law; how he'd grown up in Yorkshire and married a woman called Joy, how he'd moved at some point to Widecombe in Devon and how he'd had a career as an art dealer but was now retired. She took a guess at his age and the approximate year of his birth, as well as passing on the address of the couple's modest bungalow she'd visited just yesterday.

As she spoke, Finnbar typed the details into various social media sites and work profile sites, cross-referencing locations, dates, and companies, leap-frogging from one website to the next as he built up a clearer and clearer picture of the man she was seeking.

Lacey watched him work, astounded to see how much identifying information was scattered all over the internet, how easy it was to find, and how much could be put there without you even knowing. Around half the sites Finnbar found that mentioned Bryan were from his past employers or official art gallery events he'd attended in a professional capacity. If someone wasn't careful, it was quite possible for them to be tracked and their movements traced both geographically and through time.

Lacey shuddered at the thought of just how traceable she might be, and just how easy it might be for the art thief to track her to her home address, or Tom's, or even her mom's and Naomi's. Who knew what lengths Bryan would go to, to get his hands on that Carson Desi painting?

She also thought about how impressive it was that Edwin, as Carson Desi, had managed to disappear so thoroughly. In this age of interconnectedness, in the constant archiving of every moment, every life event, every time, place, and location, Edwin had somehow managed to take his secret identity to the grave. No wonder the forums were full of people suspecting he'd been abducted by aliens or killed by the MI5. For someone to disappear in this day and age was quite the magic act.

"Here," Finnbar announced, pointing at a phone number tracking website. "This is Bryan Vallins's home number." He scribbled it on a Post-it and handed it to her. "What are you going to do with it?"

Lacey took the paper in her hand, gazing poignantly at the sequence of numbers that were about to change the direction of her whole investigation.

"I'm going to set a trap."

CHAPTER TWENTY EIGHT

Lacey headed into the back office for privacy, clutching the sticky note Finnbar had given her. Once inside the small, gloomy room, she shut the door securely and took a deep breath to calm her racing heartbeat.

Her hands shook with nervous anticipation as she grabbed her phone and punched in the digits from the sticky note.

The dial tone seemed to go on for an agonizingly long time. Lacey waited, listening, her nerves growing with every shrill *bring-bring-bring* in her ear.

Finally, the call was answered. But it was not Bryan's voice on the line. It was Joy's.

"Hello, Vallins residence," the woman said in the same jolly tone Lacey recalled from her visit to their bungalow.

"Joy?" Lacey asked. "This is Edwin's friend, Lacey. The one with the dog."

"Oh! Lacey," the woman exclaimed. "How are you, dear? How did you get this number?"

Lacey immediately picked up on a slight difference in the tone with which she'd asked each question. The first had been the usual jovial, cordial friendliness one might expect. But the second? The second had been spoken with just an edge of suspicion.

"I was wondering if I might be able to speak to Bryan," Lacey said, sidestepping the question.

"He's not in at the moment, I'm afraid. Can I pass on a message?"

Lacey couldn't tell if she was lying or not. Her mind ticked over as she mulled on the best way to proceed. She decided to just go for it.

"I have his painting," she declared.

There was a moment of silence.

"What painting?" Joy asked, sounding confused. "Bryan doesn't deal artworks anymore. He's retired."

"It's not a work painting," Lace said. "It's a personal one."

Joy paused. "What do you mean by that?"

She was starting to sound hesitant.

"Bryan will know what I mean," Lacey said evasively.

She didn't know how much Joy really knew about anything, though she suspected it was more than her clueless act would suggest.

Joy started to huff. It sounded as if Lacey's request had flustered her.

"Look, I'm not sure what you're asking me to tell him," she said, sternly. The happy, jolly, schoolteacher persona was starting to falter.

"Tell him Lacey has his painting and if he wants it back, he'll have to come to my store in Wilfordshire."

"Is that some kind of threat?" Joy said. "Are you playing some sort of game?"

"No game," Lacey confirmed. "I can assure you, this is deadly serious."

"Fine," Joy snapped. "I'll pass your cryptic little message on. But you listen here. We're quiet people who live a quiet life, and we have no interest in getting caught up in whatever shenanigans you have going on. I wonder if you were even a friend of Edwin's in the first place. You seem like a snake to me."

And with that, she hung up.

Lacey sat back, stunned. That call hadn't gone the way she'd been expecting at all.

But she recovered her composure quickly. That was only step one of the plan. Step two would be altogether more complicated...

*

Lacey scrolled through her cell contacts until she got to DCI Lewis's entry. The female detective had shared her personal number with Lacey months ago, when it was becoming increasingly clear that Lacey was an investigative asset, even if just by lending a supportive ear to Superintendent Turner's dismissive one.

"Lacey?" came the detective's efficient-sounding voice said in her ear.

"I know who killed Edwin," Lacey blurted. "It was his brother-in-law, Bryan Vallins. They were childhood friends but the relationship soured when he worked out Edwin was Carson Desi, and I'm pretty sure Edwin marrying his sister made it even worse."

Lacey knew she was speaking at a crazy speed, but she wanted to get it all out on the table before she was shot down.

"Bryan was a struggling art dealer," she continued. "He could've profited handsomely if Edwin let him in on the secret and employed his

132

services. So when Bryan eventually found out, it caused a whole lot of bad blood between them, at least from Bryan's perspective, because Edwin's choice to remain obscure and donate all his wealth had basically meant Bryan stayed poor as well. All that rage must've spilled over when he heard about the discovery of a previously unknown Carson Desi portrait. Bryan must've been furious to learn Edwin had been sitting on a gold mine all these years."

She stopped speaking. She had more to add to support her theory, but she wanted to give Beth a chance to catch up.

On the other end of the line, Detective Lewis was completely silent.

"Lacey," she said, finally, "have you been conducting your own investigation?"

She said it with a reproachful tone. Lacey tensed. She'd been hoping Beth would find her theory compelling. While she knew her amateur sleuthing made things awkward between DCI Lewis and her superior (and not because she was wrong, but because it made things difficult with the fragile-egoed Superintendent Turner when it turned out she was right), she'd expected her to at least be on board.

"Yes," Lacey said simply. "Of course I have."

Beth let out a long, weary sigh.

"We've been looking into Bryan Vallins," she confirmed.

Lacey felt vindicated. If her own investigation was running parallel to DCI Lewis's, that was a good sign she was on the right track.

"I think I know how to get a confession out of him," Lacey continued, becoming animated again.

"So do I," Beth retorted. "With our trained officers doing their legal interviews using tried and tested interrogation methods."

Lacey frowned. So it was like that, was it? Beth was blocking her out?

"Beth," Lacey said. "You're starting to sound like Karl. It's not like you to be so resistant to my unconventional methods. Haven't I always come through for you?"

"Just let us handle this properly," Beth replied.

"No offense, but you handling it properly is too slow. Bryan is clearly desperate to get hold of the painting. If mine and Edwin's stores were ransacked, then what's next? My house? And if he doesn't find the painting there, since I don't have it, will I get bashed to death next too?"

Despite Lacey's emotive language, Beth maintained a steady tone.

133

"Your store was ransacked while you were at the Vallins property," she stated. "There's no way he was responsible."

Lacey was about to launch into her explanation about that, when it suddenly occurred to her what Beth had just let slip.

"How did you know I was at Bryan's house?" she queried.

Her question was met with silence.

"Turner had me tail you," Beth finally admitted.

That explained how he'd known where she'd been that day. But why had Beth tailed her all the way to Bryan's home without doing anything?

"Why didn't you didn't arrest me for leaving town?" Lacey asked.

"It's not a crime," Beth explained. "It just helps strengthen the prosecution's case, if it comes to that. Lack of cooperation with the police. Disregard for the law. It all helps build up a picture in a jury's eye."

That was good to know. Not that Lacey was in any hurry to violate police protocol while investigating a murder again…

"Nice costume, by the way," Beth added.

Lacey's cheeks heated up as she remembered her Gina disguise.

"*Anyway*," she said, getting back to the matter at hand, "I don't think Bryan's acting alone. He has an accomplice."

She'd been with Bryan during the time her store was ransacked, so it was physically impossible for him to be the one to have turned the place upside down. Joy couldn't be the accomplice because she was with them the whole time as well. So there had to be someone else involved. An associate from the art world? A hired hitman? Whoever Bryan had gotten to do the dirty work for him, Lacey would only find it once she was face to face with the man in question.

"I can get him to confess," Lacey continued. "I know it. And wouldn't it be good for the prosecution to have a recorded confession? Not to mention your career!"

"Lacey…" Beth interjected with a warning.

"I really think you should come over to my store and help me with this… " Lacey said.

"Lacey…" Beth said again more firmly.

"…Because I already called him to tell him to meet me here," Lacey admitted.

Beth fell silent. Finally, she sighed reluctantly. "I'll be right over."

CHAPTER TWENTY NINE

DCI Lewis arrived a short while later, plain-clothed in a dark green sweater and black pants, her dark blond hair tied in a low ponytail. There was nothing about her appearance to even vaguely suggest she was an officer of the law.

She halted in the doorway and peered around the store at the damage left from the ransacking. It was still in disarray, despite Lacey's best attempts to tidy things up.

DCI Lewis whistled. "Wow. They really did a number on you, didn't they?"

"Yup," Lacey said, sadly.

Finnbar looked up from the laptop and glanced curiously at DCI Lewis.

"You've met Beth before, haven't you?" Lacey asked him. "She's a detective with the police. She's here to help me with something."

Finnbar's eyes widened like he'd come face to face with a tarantula. Lacey remembered how anxious he was, especially around authority figures.

"Hi," he squeaked.

"Why don't you head home now?" Lacey suggested.

Finnbar didn't need much convincing. He slammed the laptop lid shut, grabbed his bag, and practically ran out of the store—not forgetting to tip his imaginary cap at Beth as he passed.

Beth frowned as she watched him go, giving him her always-suspicious cop-look, then turned back to Lacey. The two women were now alone in the store.

"I thought you'd be bringing equipment," Lacey said. "You know, tiny microphones to hide in the lampshades and stick under shelves."

"This isn't a spy movie," Beth said. "I'm an agent of the state. I can't just record people without their consent. I'd be fired for breaching the Data Protection Act."

"Oh," Lacey said, feeling silly for having even suggested it. "But I thought we were going to get a recording of his confession?"

"*We* aren't doing anything," Beth said, with emphasis. She pointed at Lacey's cell phone, poking out the top of her jeans pocket. "*You* are."

Lacey narrowed her eyes, confused. "I don't understand."

"The laws are different for private citizens," Beth explained. "You're standing in your own private property, recording for domestic purposes. The fact I have your consent to access your data, and happen to be out in the back office monitoring the whole thing, is by-the-by."

Lacey tapped her nose to indicate she understood. As long as she was the one doing the recording, Beth was safe, and the recording would be admissible in court.

The detective held her hand out for Lacey's cell phone. Lacey passed it over and watched as she took a small device out of her pocket. It looked like a smooth silver coin, with magnetic strips on a sticky side. She stuck it onto the back of Lacey's phone, then flipped it back over and opened up the cell phone's inbuilt recorder.

"Don't touch it, okay?" Beth said, as she placed the phone in the dark corner of the counter. "I'll be listening to the wiretap out back. There's quite a delay, so if you need immediate help, shout. Got it?"

"It *is* like a spy movie!" Lacey exclaimed, her eyes widening.

Beth just flashed her an annoyed look.

"How long do you think it will take for our suspect to turn up?" she asked.

"If I'm right, and Bryan is the one looking for the painting, then it shouldn't take him very long at all," Lacey replied.

Beth's expression soured. "If?" She put her hands on her hips. "Lacey, you said you were certain."

Lacey knew it would put Beth in an awkward position if she turned out to be wrong. She could only hope for both their sakes she was not.

"I am certain," she said, though her voice lacked conviction. "I think."

Beth shook her head. "You're going to get me fired one of these days," and with a final stern parting look, she headed away to shut herself in the back room out of sight.

Lacey was left to anxiously pace the shop floor, waiting to see if Bryan really would take the bait.

She tried to keep busy by tidying some more, but she was so on edge she kept visualizing Bryan creeping up on her from behind and whacking her over the head with a blunt object. In the end, she just sat watching the door instead.

Soon, the sun started to fade on the day, and the streetlamps switched on, emitting a soft yellow glow onto the recently hung autumn bunting. Lacey watched as one by one the stores closed up for the day, switching from their main lights to their neon signs in the windows. Before long, the only stores still open were hers and Tom's patisserie over the road.

Lacey wondered what he was up to. He was no doubt in the middle of some pastry extravaganza. She wondered what he'd think if he knew what *she* was up to. In the middle of a sting.

And with that thought, another wave of guilt passed over her. She had promised to keep him updated on the investigation, but she hadn't called him all day.

Just then, Lacey's phone began to ring. She jumped out of her skin.

Lacey looked over at her phone, still in the shadowy corner where Beth had placed it, its red recording light blinking away. Beth had expressly told her not to touch it. Lacey was as bad with technology as Finnbar was with hand-eye coordination. It would be just her luck to press the wrong button and waste her one opportunity to catch Edwin's killer.

She glanced over at the screen. The name *Mom* flashed at her.

Great, Lacey thought.

Now she had to weigh up infuriating her mom or temporarily pausing the recording and messing up the whole sting operation.

She shouldn't answer it. Beth had been dubious enough about helping out in the first place. Lacey getting a personal call in the middle of a stakeout probably wouldn't earn her any favors. And it would only be a wedding call, with her mom putting pressure on Lacey to make decisions she wasn't ready to make, or commit to dates she wasn't sure she could keep.

Then from the back room, she heard Beth shout, "Answer your damn phone! The noise is driving me insane!"

Lacey quickly obliged.

"Mom?" she said, answering the call tensely.

She'd better get it over and done with quickly.

"Now I know you're probably thinking about a fall wedding," Shirley said, launching immediately into it without any greetings, as she was wont to do. "Fall's your favorite season, after all. But that will mean an entire year of waiting. So I wonder if I might be able to plead the case for spring?"

Lacey opened her mouth to speak, but didn't even get a single syllable out before Shirley went off on one.

"Late winter would actually be the best, for all of us, because of Frankie's school vacation. But since that's even farther away than fall, I've decided spring break would be the next best option."

"Mom," Lacey said.

Shirley continued. "The flights wouldn't be too expensive in spring *if* you marry on the Tuesday or Wednesday before the schools go back. For some reason, Tuesdays out and Wednesdays back in are the cheapest. Obviously that would be a rather rush visit for us, but we could make it a week if you don't mind us being around that long and …"

"Mom!" Lacey snapped. She'd run out of patience. "Can we please talk about this later? I'm not ready to make any decisions yet! I don't know if I want to get married in the spring or on a Tuesday or anything! Can you please just ease off!"

Her outburst was met by silence.

"I see," her mom finally said. Her tone had changed completely. Gone was the chatty excitement of before, and in its place was a heavy disappointment. "I can tell I've caught you at a bad time. I'll leave you to it."

"Mom…" Lacey said, but the call went dead.

Lacey flopped her head into her arms. She hadn't meant to snap at her like that and she felt truly awful for it. Her mom had only been getting ahead of herself because she was excited, and Lacey had cut her down. She wondered what Beth would think of her, speaking so abruptly to her own mother that way?

Just then, Chester let out a sharp bark.

Lacey's head darted up from her arms. All worry about her mom vacated her mind. Standing outside her store was Bryan.

CHAPTER THIRTY

Lacey swallowed nervously as the man she thought had killed Edwin entered her store, the bell jangling above him. She quickly nudged her cell phone out of sight, relieved to see the recording light was still blinking away.

Bryan glanced about him as he walked along the path she'd swept through the debris. He was taller than Lacey remembered him being back at his house in Widecombe, more gangly-limbed. He had a long face with a bump in his nose, the type her father would've described as "distinguished."

"What happened here?" Bryan asked, his gray eyes darting from left to right.

He sounded innocent enough, but Lacey knew it was just an act.

"This was the emergency I got a call about yesterday," she said, keeping her voice conversational. "When I had to rush away from your house."

"Goodness," Bryan said, sounding convincingly concerned. "I'm so sorry. Edwin's store was hit yesterday as well."

Curious, Lacey thought. Why would the ransacker bring that up unprovoked? Either because he couldn't help himself, or because he was double-bluffing Lacey, trying to make himself seem like an innocent bystander.

"I heard," Lacey confirmed. "The police told me my store had been targeted along with Edwin's. The thief must be getting really desperate for the painting now."

She studied Bryan carefully, looking for any kind of reaction to her words. His face remained a blank mask. Whatever he was thinking, he was hiding it very well.

"I assumed the same," Bryn said.

He stepped closer to the counter. Chester watched him like a hawk.

"Now according to my wife, you're in possession of the painting? Is that right? I may have misunderstood your message, Joy seemed rather het up about it."

"Sorry," Lacey said. "I didn't mean to upset your wife."

Bryan flapped a dismissive hand. He was clearly far less concerned about his wife than he was about the painting.

"Well?" he pressed. "Is it true? Do you have the painting?"

"I do," Lacey said.

Bryan let out an exhalation of relief. "Thank goodness. You've no idea how worried I've been about it. I thought for sure Edwin's killer or the police would get their hands on it. And, well, that would be terrible."

Lacey wasn't entirely sure what he meant, but presumed he was talking about Edwin's secret identity being exposed. But the sort of man who could commit murder over a painting was unlikely to be the world's most attentive husband.

"You must've found a cunning hiding place if the police weren't able to find it when they searched your property," Bryan said.

"It wasn't hidden at my house," Lacey said, avoiding the question. "And anyway, how did you know the police searched my house?"

Bryan shrugged. "I don't know, actually. You must've mentioned it during your visit."

Lacey narrowed her eyes. She had no recollection of mentioning it at all. Now she had him on the ropes. She was sure of it. She just had to get him to confess.

It was time to turn up the heat.

"I'm actually surprised you didn't find it..." Lacey said, "...when you sent your accomplice to look here."

It was a risky move to make, Lacey knew. She felt her adrenaline spike.

She watched as Bryan's expression turned from confused to irritated.

"My accomplice?" he said, frowning.

Lacey's heart thumped in her chest as she raised her eyebrows. "Or whoever it was you sent here to look on your behalf."

Just then, a darkness descended over Bryan's face. His pale gray eyes seemed suddenly piercing.

"What are you suggesting?" he demanded. "That I had something to do with this?" He opened his arms wide, gesturing to the ransacked store.

He was starting to lose his cool, which meant Lacey was getting under his skin. She just had to hold her nerve now, which was easier said than done. The adrenaline was starting to make her tremble.

"Tell me," Lacey continued. "Did you recognize me when I turned up on your doorstep?"

Bryan's frown deepened. "What is this nonsense? Joy said you were being strange on the telephone. She warned me not to come here. She thinks you might have something to do with Edwin's murder, and now I'm starting to think the same. What kind of game are you playing here?"

Lacey swallowed, her throat now dry, and tried to maintain her composure. Bryan was accusing her because she had him on the ropes and he was grasping at straws.

"So you didn't watch the report about me on TV?" Lacey queried. "You weren't expecting me to turn up on your doorstep at some point anyway? And that the second you saw me there, you didn't take your chance and call your lackey to come search my store?"

"What are you accusing me of?" Bryan exclaimed. "How dare you! Do you even have the painting or are you just goading me?"

Lacey was getting to him. She just had to keep the pressure up.

"Who was it?" she demanded. "Who does your dirty work for you?"

"This is madness!" Bryan cried.

"Were you jealous of Edwin?" Lacey accused. "Had it been growing and growing ever since you were kids? He was more successful. More popular. More talented. And then he stole your sister, too. So when you discovered he was hiding a portrait of her, one potentially worth millions, you decided to steal it back off him."

"Why would I kill Edwin for a painting I always knew was there?" Bryan yelled.

"Aha!" Lacey cried. "So you admit you knew Edwin was Carson Desi all along!"

"He wasn't!" Bryan shouted back. "Diane was!"

Lacey froze, stunned. Bryan snapped his lips shut, clearly realizing he'd gotten so riled by Lacey he'd blurted out the secret he'd been keeping for all these years.

Silence fell.

"Diane is the artist?" Lacey said. "Your sister?"

Slowly, it all began to fall into place in Lacey's mind. Carson Desi wasn't Edwin's secret persona. All along, the elusive artist had been his wife Diane.

"Did Edwin know?" Lacey asked.

Bryn nodded. "We were the only people in the world who did. And we promised Diane we'd take that secret to the grave. Edwin did. And I'll be damned if I'm the one who breaks her secret."

That's when Lacey noticed the glint in his eye. She'd worked out the identity of Carson Desi, and now Bryan was going to have to make sure she never told another living soul.

He was going to kill her, just like he killed Edwin.

Panic made Lacey's throat constrict, so tight it felt like hands around her throat. She thought desperately of Beth Lewis in the back room, waiting for her to shout for help before charging out. But Lacey's heart was racing too fast for her to catch her breath and scream. Her only hope was that the delay in the recording didn't take too long.

"Edwin broke his promise when he sold me the painting," Lacey stammered breathlessly. "Is that why you killed him?"

"I didn't kill Edwin," Bryan stated. "Edwin kept his promise to the end. You're the one who's been messing everything up. Digging and digging and digging. You're the one who's threatening to ruin everything. Edwin kept his end of the bargain, but now that you know, I have no choice but to make sure I keep mine."

He reached into his top pocket. Was he reaching for a gun?

Lacey put her hands over her head. "Don't hurt me!" she squeaked.

Bryan froze. "Hurt you?" he echoed, looking horrified.

Lacey could feel her hands shaking in their cactus position beside her head.

"I'm not going to hurt you!" Bryan said, looking utterly horrified.

"You don't have a gun?"

"Goodness, no!" Bryan exclaimed. He removed his hand from his pocket. He was holding a checkbook. "I'm here to negotiate with you. How much for your secrecy?"

Lacey couldn't believe it. She'd thought Bryan was going to kill her. Instead, he wanted to pay her to stay silent?

"I don't understand," Lacey said. "You... you weren't the one to kill Edwin?"

Bryan shook his head emphatically. "No. It wasn't me."

Suddenly Lacey realized she'd gotten it all wrong.

Just then, Beth Lewis burst out of the back room into the main store, gun raised and pointed at Bryan.

"Drop your weapon!" she cried. "I'm an officer of the law!"

142

Bryan's hands immediately went into the air. He looked utterly stunned.

Lacey immediately realized the mistake and shook her head. "No, Beth. It's all a misunderstanding. I'm sorry. Bryan isn't the killer."

Still in her shooting poise, Beth's gaze went up to Bryan's hands, to the innocuous checkbook he was holding.

"You don't have a weapon?" she asked.

Bryan shook his head. "Just a checkbook," he said.

Beth stayed in the same posture for a moment, scanning her surroundings as the little headphone in her ear brought her up to speed.

A look of utter humiliation overcame her features. She moved out of her shooting stance and quickly stashed her gun back in its concealed holster. She coughed awkwardly.

"I—er, I'm extremely sorry about that," she said to Bryan.

His hands were still straight up in the air. "Can I—?"

"Yes. Yes, put your hands down," Beth said.

She looked too awkward to even meet his eye. Instead, she fixed her furious gaze on Lacey.

"You were wrong," she said.

Lacey's cheeks burned. "Beth, I'm sorry."

But Beth wasn't sticking around to listen to her apology. Without another word, she turned and marched out of the store.

CHAPTER THIRTY ONE

Lacey popped a cup of coffee on the table next to Bryan, her heart rate finally back to normal. She took the stool beside him at the counter.

"How are you doing?" she asked.

Bryan took his coffee and nodded. "I think I'm okay. It's not every day I get a gun pointed in my face."

Lacey felt terrible for what had happened earlier.

"Help me understand," she said. "Your sister was the artist all along?"

"That's right. Carson Desi. Diane Cross."

"It's an anagram," Lacey realized.

"Her idea," Bryan said, with a mournful smile on his lips. "She loved things like that. Puzzles and riddles and the like. Of course, she was young, radical, and a lot more naive when she picked the name. She thought it would be funny to toy with the male-dominated artworld by using a male pseudonym. She didn't realize she was about to become one of the country's most cherished artists. I think, with hindsight, she may well have picked something else that had no chance of being traced back to her."

Lacey listened attentively. She calculated back in her mind the bits of information she'd cobbled together so far.

"Correct me if I'm wrong, but wasn't she still Diane Vallins when she was producing her artwork? She and Edwin didn't marry until after she quit being Carson Desi."

Bryan smiled. "Goodness. You have been doing your research, haven't you?"

Lacey shrugged. "Sleuthing is kind of my thing."

Bryan took a sip of coffee. It was clear to Lacey that talking about his late sister was difficult for him, and she appreciated him giving her his time, especially considering she'd not that long earlier accused him of a terrible crime.

"Diane's career took off during her first marriage," Bryan explained. "She created the Carson Desi persona when she was Diane

Milton. The fact she made her pseudonym an anagram of a different man's name tells you everything you need to know, really."

"She loved Edwin," Lacey offered.

Bryan nodded. "Precisely. We all grew up together in Leeds, me and Diane, Edwin and Joy. I always loved Joy and Joy always loved me. Diane always loved Edwin, and Edwin always loved Diane. Yet Joy and I married, and Diane married another man."

Lacey didn't need to ask why Diane had made her fateful decision. She understood firsthand how a person could end up making the wrong choice when it came to matters of romance. She'd been married to the wrong man for fourteen years.

Bryan continued his story. "The self-portrait was actually created very early in her career. She was about to release it when she hit the big time. It's a relief she didn't. It wouldn't have taken long for people to find out she was the model, and hypothesize she was also the artist. The mystery of Carson Desi was almost over before it began."

Lacey wondered how different things would've been if Diane's identity had never been concealed. Would interest in her have petered out over the years, or would she still be one of the country's most celebrated artists? And, painfully, would Edwin still be alive now?

"Why was Diane so secretive about her identity?" Lacey asked. "Beyond enjoying toying with her fans and tricking the art world, why was it so important to her to stay completely anonymous? I hope you don't take this as a criticism, but don't you think she took it to extremes? Roping you all in as well? Making you jump through all these hoops, even after her death?"

Bryan took some time before he answered her. He was clearly deliberating over something.

"Diane's first husband wasn't a good man," he said, carefully. "He was one of those men who thought women should be in the kitchen baking cakes, rather than earning more money than them and achieving more things than they could. Diane was concerned that if he'd worked it out who she was, he would put her in an early grave."

Lacey let the words sink in. Her chest tightened with empathy. "Was he violent toward her?"

Bryan nodded, the pain in his gray eyes evident. He swallowed hard, making his Adam's apple bob up and back down. "He was a truly vicious human."

Lacey shuddered. She felt terrible for the young Diane and all she'd endured.

145

Lacey thought about the Carson Desi portraits she knew of. Diane's ability to capture emotion was unparalleled. In her self-portrait, Lacey had pin-pointed a knowing look in her eye, one that contained such complexity it could be read in several different ways. Lacey knew now that it was the look of a woman in hiding, of a woman suppressed, her wings clipped. But the strength was still there. She'd not been battered down. She was going to fight, when the time was right. That woman was saying, "Just watch me."

"Were you her agent?" Lacey asked.

"Yes. It made sense to keep it in the family. I can't say I have much of an eye for art myself, but I was able to fake my way through."

Lacey almost chuckled. She'd thought Bryan had been the ambitious one who'd wanted fame and fortune, but he was just as humble as Edwin. He'd fallen into his career to help his sister, not because he had lofty aspirations.

"So that's how you managed to keep her identity a secret from everyone?"

He nodded. "Precisely. And by making sure the self-portrait remained hidden. You should see the extent that some of these forum obsessives go to. They can find signs in anything. We thought if anyone ever saw the painting and worked out who the model was, they'd quickly work out the anagram. And if her first husband got wind of her using an anagram of Diane Cross, he'd probably kill the lot of us, me, Edwin, and Joy included."

Lacey felt terrible for Diane. Despite being a uniquely gifted artist, her first go at life had been awful. But then she'd left and married Edwin, living a quiet, unassuming life in the countryside. Her second go at it had seemingly worked out much better for her.

"How did Diane and Edwin finally get together?" Lacey asked, recalling her theory about Bryan's fury over the betrayal.

"That's a story I don't fully know," Bryan said. "Diane refused to give me the details, and all Edwin would tell me is that she turned up on his doorstep in the middle of the night, and by the time dawn rose they'd put three hundred miles of distance between them and Yorkshire."

Lacey whistled. It was quite the story. Diane must have been truly terrified of her first husband to flee in the middle of the night and travel half the country.

"Could Diane's first husband be the killer?" Lacey asked.

146

Bryan shook his head. "He's dead. He passed away not that long after Diane left."

"You must've been relieved."

"Oh we were," Bryan said. "I'd not seen her for years by that point. He'd kept her from her family, you see. So when Edwin called to tell us they were together and in *Exeter* of all places, well, Joy and I packed the house and moved down within the week. It was a wonderful reunion, believe you me. But Diane was changed." He sighed sadly.

"Changed how?"

He flashed a mournful look at Lacey. "She'd lost something of herself. And not just that she quit painting. It was like part of her had been taken away, and we never got it back."

"I'm sorry," Lacey said.

She patted his hand sympathetically.

He smiled morosely. "Edwin loved her all the same."

"That's beautiful. They were very lucky to have found their way back to each other after everything." She sipped her coffee. "But I guess what I still don't understand, is why, even after her ex-husband had passed away, Diane still kept her identity such a secret. She wasn't in danger anymore, was she?"

"Well, part of it was just the way she was. Quiet. Unassuming. Fame and fortune never interested her. But the other part... honestly, I don't think she ever truly believed she was safe from him," Bryan said. "She had all her art pieces anonymously donated, apart from the portrait, of course. She only took as much money as she needed to live a modest, comfortable life and donated the rest."

"And you and Edwin kept her secret all these years. Even after her death."

"Yes. Joy and I are the only people left alive who know Carson Desi's true identity. Well, us, and now you."

It was a huge secret to suddenly be responsible for, Lacey thought.

"I won't tell anyone," she promised.

"I know," Bryan said.

He stood from his stool, his coffee cup now drained. "I'd best get back to Joy. She might think you've killed me."

"I'm so sorry about that," Lacey said, quickly. "For suspecting you."

Bryan chuckled. "I'm actually touched to know someone cares that much about Edwin. Stay safe, though, Lacey. Whoever killed him is still out there. Until we know where the painting is, we're both in danger."

With that, he left.

Lacey sank back onto her stool, Bryan's story weighing on her.

Though she had more of the puzzle pieces than she'd started with, she was more confused than ever. Her hunch had been wrong. All of Bryan's peculiarities weren't because he was the killer, but because of all the hoops he was jumping through to protect his sister's identity.

And that meant she was back to square one.

Suddenly, Lacey noticed the blinking red light in the shadowy corner of the counter.

The recording device! It had been on this whole time!

Panic overcame her. The whole conversation with Bryan had been committed to a piece of technology, with the internet and a wiretap going to the police. With everything she'd discovered during Finnbar's internet sleuthing, things committed to physical existence had a way of being leaked, found, distributed, copied, amplified. What if the crazed internet forum people found their way to it?

She quickly deleted the recording. But what about Beth? Had she overhead everything through her wiretap? And considering how badly things had gone earlier, would Beth Lewis ever do her any favors ever again?

With a sinking feeling, Lacey realized she had a hell of a lot of groveling to do.

CHAPTER THIRTY TWO

As soon as Bryan was gone, Lacey hurried around the store checking all the doors and windows were locked. Since he wasn't the killer, that meant whoever was, was still on the loose. And if they thought she might have the painting, then that meant she was still in danger.

Chester watched her curiously as she rushed about securing the windows. It only occurred to her then that he hadn't barked at Bryan the whole time he'd been in the store. She should've realized from Chester's silence that Bryan wasn't going to hurt her. Chester was usually a very good judge of character.

With the store secure, the next pressing issue on Lacey's agenda was to patch things up with DCI Lewis and try to convince her to erase the wiretap data. Deleting everything entirely was the only way to make sure Diane's secret identity wasn't accidentally leaked somehow.

She dialed the detective's number, feeling apprehensive.

"What?" Beth asked gruffly as she answered the call.

"First of all, I'm really sorry," Lacey began.

"You're sorry?" Beth immediately interjected. "Okay, great. That makes everything all better then."

It took Lacey a second to realize she was being sarcastic. Despite having lived in England for the good part of a year, she often forgot about the general population's penchant for sarcasm.

She sighed. "Go on then. Let me have it. If it will make you feel better."

"It won't," Beth snapped back. "Not having wasted an entire day pursuing the wrong line of inquiry would make me feel better, but since you can't turn back the hands of time, I guess that one's off the table."

Lacey winced. Beth was beyond furious, and Lacey couldn't blame her. She'd led her down the wrong path. And who knows, perhaps if Lacey hadn't meddled and just left Detective Lewis to do what she did best—detective work—then Edwin's killer may well have been caught, and be sitting in a jail cell this very moment.

"Do you know how much crap Superintendent Turner is going to give me over this?" Beth continued. She clearly wasn't done with her chastisement. "I have a briefing meeting in five minutes." She lowered her voice. "And I am going to get my ass whooped."

"Can't you say you spent the day surveilling Bryan Vallins before striking him off your perp list?" Lacey said, hopefully. "You did say he was a suspect."

"Don't tell me how to do my job," Beth said, thinly.

She was starting to sound like Superintendent Turner. That was one of his catchphrases.

Lacey knew she wasn't going to get anywhere with Beth right now. She'd royally screwed up and it wouldn't get any better until the case was solved. And that felt like something Lacey was even farther from achieving now she'd burnt her only bridge in the police department.

As much as Lacey wanted to patch things up with Beth, it was quite obvious that she wasn't going to be able to do it during their telephone call. So she may as well just bite the bullet and do what she'd been intending to do when she made the call in the first place.

"I need to ask you a favor," she said.

Beth let out a laugh of derision. "Are you being serious right now?"

Lacey had been fully expecting Beth's incredulous response, but she still recoiled from her fury. She hated letting people down. Being an ever-constant disappointment to her mother had really drilled that one into her.

"I need you to wipe the tapes," Lacey said.

"From earlier?" Beth asked. "It's already done."

"Really?"

Lacey was taken aback. That had been far too easy. She'd been expecting some push back from Detective Lewis. Or a lecture at the very least.

"Do you really think I want my superior knowing I helped instigate a failed sting operation?" She was whisper-shouting now. "Or that I pulled my weapon on an innocent man! God no. I stopped the device as soon as I left and wiped the lot."

"Oh," Lacey said. "Good." She looked at the shiny coin thing still attached to the back of her cell phone. "Do you want your thingy back?"

"You can post it," Beth said.

"Okay," Lacey said, meekly. "I really am sorry."

"It's not your fault," Beth replied. "I should never have trusted a civilian."

And with that, she hung up.

150

Ouch, Lacey thought. Beth's parting comment had been particularly cold. She wasn't exactly a friend, but they were friendly enough, and being demoted to "civilian" stung. Beth really was starting to sound like Superintendent Turner. Next she'd be calling Chester Rex or Fido or Lassie.

At the thought of her pup, Lacey looked over at Chester, resting in his basket. He raised his eyes to meet hers.

"Come on, boy," she said. "Let's get out of here."

She'd had about enough of the day as she could stand.

*

It was pitch-black as Lacey left her store. The shift in the atmosphere was immediately apparent. Gone was the cool stillness of a late summer evening, and in its place was the chill of fall.

Across the street, Lacey saw that the lights in the patisserie were now off. Tom must've locked up and gone home while she was chatting with Bryan. She'd been quietly hoping her fiancé would be working late so she could walk straight into the comforting, buttery-scented patisserie and have him wrap her up in his warm, strong arms, and protect her from the big bad guy who was still on the prowl. So much for her earlier confidence that she could hold her own. Knowing the killer and ransacker was still on the loose had left her feeling totally rattled.

Well, if Tom couldn't be there in person, Lacey decided, she'd have to settle for the next best thing.

She took out her cell, dialed his number, and wedged the phone under her ear. As the dial tone sounded, she twisted her key to operate the store's motorized steel shutters. They began to slowly rattle into place, screeching as they descended.

"Hi, hon," Tom said, brightly as he answered the call.

His happy tone seemed about a million miles away from how Lacey was feeling.

"Hey," she said.

"What's that noise?" Tom asked.

"It's the shutters. I'm just locking up," Lacey told him.

She willed the shutters to hurry up. They always seemed to take forever when she was in a hurry.

"Why are you working so late?" Tom asked.

"I have a lot of tidying up to do."

"Where are Finnbar and Gina? Why aren't they helping you?"

"I gave them some time off," Lacey explained. "I need to inventory everything and I don't trust them not to mess it up."

At last the shutters hit the floor. Lacey removed her phone from where she'd wedged it between her ear and shoulder, and began to walk toward the side street where her car was parked. Chester trotted along beside her, his claws clicking on the cobblestones.

"Lacey, I hope you're not getting all control-freaky again," she heard Tom say in her ear. "We both agreed to hire extra staff specifically so we could have a better work/life balance."

"I know, I know," Lacey said. "And I'm not getting all 'control-freaky,' I promise. The tidy-up just has to be done meticulously for insurance reasons."

That was true, at least. Tom didn't need to know that the other main reason she'd given her employees time off was because she didn't want to put them in harm's way. She knew if she told him that, he'd just turn it back on her, and question her about why she felt there was such a thing as "harm's way" to put anyone into, why she felt it was okay for that person to be herself.

"Anyway, I'm done for the day," she added. "I'm just getting to the car."

Her pale silvery-brown Volvo had just come into sight up ahead, parked in its normal spot. None of the other business proprietors' cars that would usually be parked against the curbs were there, since all the other stores had been locked up and everyone else had gone home. The only other vehicle was a Devon Gas van parked a little way down the road from her own.

"Good," Tom said. "You know I worry about you. Especially after what happened last night."

"I know," Lacey said. She used her car key to unlock the driver's side door. Chester muscled his way past her and jumped in. It was a naughty habit she'd not yet had the time to train out of him.

"I was wondering if you could come over tonight?" Lacey asked, sliding into her car, gently shunting Chester over to the passenger side.

Tom paused. "Of course. Why? Has something happened?"

He was becoming perceptive, Lacey realized. It started around about the time they'd gotten engaged, in fact. Tom was usually a bit of a head-in-the-clouds type, far too happy-go-lucky to pick up on any nasty undercurrents or bad vibes. But by the sounds of things, Lacey's super-sensitive perceptiveness was starting to rub off on him.

"Lacey?" Tom pressed. "What's going on?"

Lacey quickly locked her car door, then leaned over and double-checked the lock on Chester's side.

"It's nothing," she told him.

She didn't want him to know what she'd been up to with Detective Lewis and Bryan, not just because she was embarrassed about the failed sting operation, but because she knew she'd done something reckless and potentially dangerous, and Tom would disapprove. But she'd worried him, and she had to give him something or he'd never drop it.

Luckily, the disastrous telephone conversation with her mother earlier popped into her mind.

"It's my mom," she blurted. "She's being pushy about the wedding. She has so many questions and I don't even know where to begin."

Even though it was half true, Lacey still felt bad for lying to her fiancé by omission.

"Ohhh, you want to do *wedding planning* tonight?" Tom said, sounding like he'd cracked the case. "Why didn't you just say?"

He chuckled and Lacey responded with a limp laugh.

"Heh. Yeah. You figured me out."

"Well, of course I want to come over tonight to do wedding planning!" Tom exclaimed, returning to his bright self. "But I have some invoicing paperwork that I really have to get done. I can do it at your place, or I can get it done beforehand so we can have the rest of the evening clear?"

Lacey immediately felt bad about having interrupted his evening of paperwork. She knew far too well how hard Tom worked, up at the crack of dawn, baking until dusk, often working seven days a week. The last thing he needed was for Lacey to be all clingy.

"You know what," she said, shaking herself off. "Just come over when you're free. Get your stuff done first."

"In that case, I'll be round at about nine. Are you sure that's okay with you?"

"It's fine," Lacey assured him.

She'd had enough of feeling like a trembling damsel in distress. It was time to start acting like the strong woman she usually was.

She'd only have a couple of hours to kill on her own before he was there. What was the worst that could happen?

CHAPTER THIRTY THREE

Lacey felt marginally better after her phone call with Tom. She started the engine and pulled away from the curb.

The Wilfordshire high street felt particularly eerie as she drove. All the stores were shut, and though the streetlamps were all on, they were emitting a strange, muddy yellow glow. The effect was that each lamppost had a pool of light beneath it, but in the spaces either side it was pitch-black. Every time an innocent pedestrian stepped out of one of the dark spots, Lacey jumped.

So much for shaking it off, she thought.

She reached the end of the high street, where the Coach and Horses pub stood. She was surprised to see none of the picnic benches outside occupied, and the main doors closed. The pub was usually a glowing beacon of light, but the cooler weather had evidently driven all the patrons inside.

She turned onto the shoreside road. The beach was equally deserted, and the ocean's black waves were churning. Even the cliffs ahead of her seemed imposing rather than comforting.

"I really am on edge, aren't I?" she said to Chester.

But it was understandable. Her theory about Bryan being the killer was wrong. Whoever had murdered Edwin was still on the loose, and they were still on the hunt for the Carson Desi painting. They must be getting desperate by now, if a murder and two ransackings had failed to produce it.

Lacey was relieved when she finally pulled onto the cliff road and crawled up to her cottage. She parked and hurried to her front door, Chester running along with her to keep up. She fished her Rapunzel key out of her pocket, twisted it in the lock, and barged inside her home, slamming the door behind her. She scraped across the heavy bolt, then hurried to the back door and slid the deadbolt into place. Then, just to be extra certain, she checked the French doors on her bedroom balcony were as secure as possible, before doing a final lap of the place to make sure every single window was securely locked.

Only then did she allow herself to flop onto the coach.

How had Diane done it all those years? she wondered. Keeping her identity secret and maintaining her anonymity to stay safe from her violent ex-husband? Lacey had been doing it for a day and she already felt like she was reaching the edge of her sanity. No wonder Diane had come home changed. No wonder she always felt like she had to look over her shoulder, even after her husband's death. It was almost impossible to relax when it felt like someone was after you.

Lacey also wondered how Diane and managed to hide her art career from her first husband. For some years at least, she'd continued producing work as Carson Desi right under his nose and without him ever suspecting.

Just then, Lacey heard a knock at the door and jumped a mile. She pressed a hand to her racing heart and glanced at the clock. Five to nine.

"That'll be Tom," she told Chester.

She shook herself and headed for the door, her loyal English Shepherd in tow.

But when she pulled open the front door, it was not Tom standing on her doorstep. It was a man, with dark hair and a short, stocky build. He was wearing blue workman's overalls, which did nothing to help flatter his figure, and he was clutching a metal toolbox. Lacey could see his thick dark arm hair reached all the way down to his knuckles. The hairs on the back of Lacey's neck immediately stood to attention.

"Evening, love," the man said, brightly. "Sorry to trouble you. I'm from Devon Gas. I need to do an inspection of your gas line."

He looked vaguely familiar to Lacey. Perhaps he'd been to her house before to sort out the gas on the old property when she'd first moved in? Still, that wasn't enough to calm her nerves.

"Isn't it a bit late for an inspection?" she probed.

"Apologies for the unsociable hour," the man replied with a chuckle. "There was a leak down at the high street earlier this evening. Nothing to worry about, but we need to inspect all the lines in the area to make sure there are no other faults."

Lacey remembered the Devon Gas van she'd seen parked around the corner of her store. Suspiciously, she cast her eyes over the man's shoulder and saw a matching van parked in her driveway, the Devon Gas insignia on its side.

"Can I see your ID?" Lacey asked.

"Course," he said, without missing a beat.

He fished his lanyard out from inside the zipper of his Devon Gas jacket and held it up to her.

Hi! I'm Shaun! it read. *My employee number is 46512.*

Lacey had a particular distaste for the way companies tried to make themselves sound like your friend. She wondered exactly who would be ingratiated by such a strategy. She certainly wasn't, and its colloquial tone did nothing to ease her paranoia.

"Do you mind waiting a moment?" she said.

"Go ahead," Shaun replied, smiling.

She shut the door on the maintenance man and dialed Devon Gas. It was something her mother always did after their father left and it was just the three of them alone in the apartment. Back then, Lacey would cringe with embarrassment and wonder how her mother never seemed even remotely self-conscious doing it. Now, she totally got it.

"I'd like to check an employee number," Lacey told the customer service rep who picked up the call.

"Go ahead," said the tired, bored-sounding young man on the other end of the line.

"It's 46512."

She listened to the sound of keyboard keys tapping. A moment later, the boy spoke.

"Yup. That's one of ours."

"Thanks," Lacey said.

She ended the call and was left wondering if a lack of professionalism was some kind of company strategy she didn't understand.

Anyway, the point was that Shaun the gas engineer was legit, and Lacey breathed a sigh of relief. She opened the door again. Shaun turned and smiled at her.

"All good?" he asked.

"Yes. Sorry about that," she said.

"No problem," he said, jovially. "All part of the job. May I?" He pointed through the door.

Lacey opened it wider. "Of course."

But as she moved away to allow Shaun entrance, she almost tripped on Chester. Her dog had quietly come up behind her and was sitting alert, ears pointed to the ceiling. He *yapped* at her clumsiness.

"I'm sorry," she told him. "I didn't see you there. You shouldn't creep up on people like that."

"Ah," the gas man said, looking at Chester. "Do you mind popping the pooch out the back for me? I have a bit of a phobia."

"Chester won't hurt you," Lacey said.

"I got bit as a boy," Shaun explained. "As they say, once bitten, twice shy."

"Okay, sure. No problem," Lacey said. She turned to Chester. "Come on, boy. Let's go."

Chester emitted a grumble of annoyance. She couldn't blame him. First he was kept away from all that exciting police business, and now he couldn't even watch all this exciting gas leak business! The poor pup was being excluded from all the "fun."

She opened the kitchen door and gestured him inside. But Chester stood his ground, letting out a low growl of complaint.

"Are you annoyed with me for treading on you?" Lacey asked him. "It wasn't personal. Now can you please get in?"

Chester snarled. Lacey was taken aback. That wasn't like him at all. He was on edge as well.

Just then, Lacey realized why. Her heart began to race. She peered back over her shoulder to where Shaun the gas engineer was standing in the hallway, waiting patiently. Chester didn't trust him. And neither did she.

She crouched down.

"Listen," she whispered to Chester. "In. Wait."

Chester whined. Lacey could hardly communicate the finer details with him through the few words he understood, so she repeated again firmly. "In. Wait."

Chester obeyed. But by the way he was holding his ears and tail as he slunk inside, she could tell he was thoroughly displeased with her plan.

Lacey pulled the kitchen door shut, but made sure not to click the latch fully into place, leaving it just ajar enough not to be spotted from afar, but so Chester could get out easily.

With her heart still racing, she returned to the corridor where Shaun was patiently waiting.

"Sorry about that," she said.

Her voice sounded stilted to her ears, but Shaun didn't seem to pick up on the change.

"No problem," he replied. "I'll start by checking your meter. Is the box under the stairs?"

"Yes, it's in the cupboard."

She showed him the way, watching him like a hawk the whole time.

Shaun got his little flashlight out from his pocket and went inside the cupboard, whistling a jaunty tune as he worked.

"Nice house you've got here," came his voice from the darkness. "I'd kill for a place like this. I don't have the cash for it on my salary, though. Gas engineer and all that. I expect you inherited it, did you?"

"No actually," Lacey said, her gaze fixed to the bald patch on the back of his head. "I bought it myself."

She heard scrabbling noises coming from inside the cupboard—the sound of the metal toolbox opening, something from inside being removed. Her anxiety spiked.

"Huh," came his voice from the depths of the cupboard. "I figured you must've had a helping hand along the way. But I suppose antiquing pays well enough."

Lacey went cold all over. She'd never said anything about working in antiques.

That was all the confirmation she needed. Her fear was justified. Shaun knew who she was.

At that moment, he turned from the cupboard. He was brandishing a hammer.

"Do what I say and no one gets hurt."

CHAPTER THIRTY FOUR

Lacey stepped back, terrified, her hands in the air, her gaze laser-focused on the hammer Shaun was wielding in his hands.

She couldn't believe what was happening. Shaun wasn't an engineer from Devon Gas. He was some kind of home invader. But she'd been so careful! She'd double-checked his credentials! Yet somehow, despite all her precautions, she was now in danger. Grave danger.

"Take anything," she said, frantically. "Just don't hurt me. Please."

Somehow, in the midst of her desperate panic, Lacey was able to think clearly. Two things about this scenario were working in her favor: Chester down the hallway behind the unlocked kitchen door; and Tom, who was due to arrive any minute. If she could stall the hammer-wielding maniac until Tom arrived, she might just make it out of this unscathed.

But stalling a hammer-wielding maniac was easier said than done.

"Wh—who are you?" Lacey asked, her voice quivering with fear.

Shaun pointed at his lanyard, with the Devon Gas insignia.

"I'm just a humble gas engineer," he said, with a shrug. "A ghost. An unseen cog in the machine, drifting quietly through my uneventful life."

Lacey frowned with bewilderment. What was this man's deal? He clearly had some kind of prejudice against people he perceived to be richer than himself; he'd commented on her house, her wealth, and made assumptions about how she'd come to own her property. He'd even said he'd kill to own a house like hers. Was that why he'd targeted her? Had he been watching her from his work van, while he'd been parked around the corner of her store? Had he followed her home from work, presuming that because she worked in antiques, she'd live in a rich house he could rob?

"This way," Shaun commanded.

He shoved her with the hammer, shunting her in the direction of the living room. Lacey's legs trembled beneath her as she entered the living room.

"What do you want?" Lacey asked, fearfully, her hands still raised above her head.

"I'm surprised you haven't figured it out yet," came Shaun's toying reply.

He poked her in the back with the hammer, as if to indicate he wanted her to sit. Lacey did, sinking into her couch.

She peered up at him, studying his features. She'd thought they were familiar before.

But now, she was looking at him closely and fully, and it hit Lacey where she recognized him from. The dark eyes. The "distinguished" nose. She recognized him from the portrait of Diane. They shared the same features.

The realization hit her like a ton of bricks.

"You're Diane's son," Lacey gasped.

Shaun clapped slowly. "Surprise."

He *had* followed her home from work, Lacey realized. Not because he thought she was a rich antiquarian worth burglarizing, but because he thought she had the painting. He was the one who'd ransacked her store looking for it. Who'd ransacked Edwin's. Who'd murdered him…

But Bryan had never said a word about having a nephew, nor Edwin a child. Shaun wasn't in any of the family photographs on the mantelpiece either. That could only mean one thing. Shaun was Diane's son, from her first marriage, to the violent man she'd fled from, and *no one* knew he existed.

Piece by piece it all fit together in Lacey's mind.

That's why Diane had come home changed. Why it seemed to everyone like she'd lost a part of herself. Because in fleeing her violent husband, she'd left her own child behind.

Shaun's expression twisted into a sneer.

"She was very good at keeping secrets, was my mother," he said.

From the vitriol with which he said the word *mother*, Lacey could tell there was clearly no love lost between them.

"No one knew about me," Shaun continued. "Not even her family. She didn't want them judging her."

"Judging her for what?" Lacey asked.

She couldn't quite wrap her head around it all. It wasn't like Diane had Shaun out of wedlock. Even if she had, her family didn't seem like the sort to shun a loved one for breaking a social taboo.

"For abandoning her child," Shaun said. "For taking her money and leaving me and dad destitute. You know, he never got over his broken

160

heart. He took his own life in the nineties. *That's* the real legacy of the world-famous *Carson Desi.*"

Lacey wanted to tell Shaun her mother had no choice. That she was running for her life. That her father had been the one to drive her away in the first place. But the threat of the weapon in his hand terrified her into silence.

"What kind of woman abandons her kids for a penniless bric-a-brac seller?" he spat.

His dad must've gaslit him. He must've been fed lies his whole life about Diane's abandonment. The cruel bully had given Diane no choice but to abandon her child, and then he'd vilified her for it and turned her son against her. It was too sad to believe.

"She didn't even tell Edwin about you?" Lacey asked.

"Of course not," Shaun snapped. "Edwin thought my mother could do no wrong. He thought the sun shone out of her backside." A smirk played across Shaun's lips. "You should've seen his face when I told him who I was, and he realized his beloved wife was a heartless monster all along."

Lacey felt a painful pressure on her chest as she pictured Edwin's last moments.

From Shaun's twisted perspective, Edwin was the reason his mother had abandoned him. That was the reason why the ransacking at Edwin's store had culminated in his murder. Because Shaun hadn't been able to contain his rage when finally faced with the person he blamed for all his life's misgivings. He'd tormented Edwin before killing him, by revealing his identity, revealing, in turn, that Diane had lied to Edwin for all their years of marriage. And he'd done it just to watch him suffer.

But how did he track his mom down? Lacey wondered. *How did he know she was the famous reclusive painter?*

She'd hidden herself so thoroughly a whole bunch of obsessive internet sleuths hadn't found her. How had Shaun done what others had failed to?

"How did you find her?" Lacey asked, hoping his own arrogance would be his downfall. "Your mother? And how did you know she was Carson Desi?"

"I didn't," Shaun said. "She found me. It was after she got her cancer diagnosis. She knew she didn't have long left. She found me and told me everything. Or at least her version. When she told me she was Carson Desi, for a second I thought I was rich. At last. After being poor my whole life, I thought I'd finally won the lottery. But then she said that there was nothing left for me to inherit. Everything she hadn't spent she'd donated! *Donated!* To charity! As if her own living flesh and blood didn't deserve a single penny!" He spat the words out bitterly. "All I got was a paltry sum for signing the gag order."

Greed. Money. That was all that mattered to Shaun Milton.

Lacey realized then that the motive she'd attributed to Bryan fit perfectly for Shaun. *Shaun* was the one who felt bitter about being lied to, being left out of the secret, being denied the riches of Carson Desi. As far as he saw it, his mother's decision had left him a poor, insignificant "ghost."

"So when I saw the news report that a Carson Desi had been discovered," Shaun continued, "I realized she'd lied." His voice turned vicious. His eyes looked crazed. "Even on her deathbed my mother lied to me! She fobbed me off with a paltry silence payout when all along there was an entire fortune I was being kept from."

His knuckles turned white from how hard he was clenching the hammer.

"Do you know how hard it is to break those contracts? There's a whole bloody team of lawyers protecting Carson Desi's legacy. Do you know how completely screwed you are if you even say a word? I tried dropping hints on the forums, anonymously, but I got shot down every time, and then I'd get a call from some anonymous legal team threatening me. Lovely woman, my mother," he added with dry sarcasm.

"You see what she's driven me to?" he demanded. "I can't legally take what's mine, so I have to steal. She's turned me into a thief."

His twisted logic was astounding. No one had forced him to become a thief and killer. He'd chosen to take that path all by himself.

Lacey also suspected his story about the gag order and lawyers was way overblown. Shaun didn't just want the painting for the fortune, but for fame. He didn't want to just earn money from being Carson Desi's son, he wanted to be known as Carson Desi's son. But no one would ever believe him. No newspaper would print his story if it risked them being sued for libel. In fact, they probably received a bunch of calls every year from people claiming to be the long-lost child of Carson Desi. With no traceable evidence, he'd be dismissed as just another quack.

Lacey realized then that Shaun's actions were so much more than just greed. He'd never be able to claim the painting for himself legally.

His solution—to murder Edwin for it—was obviously crazy, but he was clearly unhinged. He had a psychological hang-up about his mother choosing a bric-a-brac seller over her own child. And if he couldn't claim his true identity, then he'd invent a whole new one for himself by becoming a murderer. At least then he'd become somebody, rather than being a nobody, like he felt.

"I'm here for the painting," Shaun said. "Where is it?"

Lacey shook her head. "I don't have it."

"Lies. Edwin told me you did, right before I lost it. It's amazing how quickly people squeal when you brandish a hammer at them." He waved it for emphasis.

Lacey swallowed hard. She didn't believe him. He was trying to turn her against Edwin so she'd be more inclined to save herself.

"I don't have it," she said again, more firmly. "If I did, I'd have no reason not to give it to you. I don't need it, or want it. I think it should belong to you."

Shaun hesitated. "What?"

"The painting. It should belong to you. It's the least you deserve, after everything you've been through. It's your inheritance, after all. You should be lying on a beach in the Bahamas right now instead of working as a gas engineer."

Shaun sneered. "Like hell you do. You're just saying that."

He was right. She was being disingenuous, and he could tell. If she really wanted Shaun to spare her, she'd have to dig a little deeper, right down to the part of herself that she recognized in him.

"I—I know what it's like to be abandoned," she said, her voice hitching with pain. "My dad. He abandoned me. I know what it's like to be brushed aside. Discarded. Forgotten about."

Shaun faltered.

Lacey could tell she was giving him pause for thought. She was speaking to the vulnerable child inside of him, telling that little boy who was so full of pain that she understood him. She could only pray it would be enough to make him see that harming her wouldn't fix it. It wouldn't stop the pain.

"You're just saying that," Shaun said, but his voice lacked conviction.

"I'm not," Lacey said, boldly. "I know what it's like to wonder why you weren't enough to make them stay. That pain doesn't get better. Ever."

She wasn't excusing Shaun's behavior, she just had an insight as to where it had come from. Diane's abandonment planted the seed, and over the years it had festered. If she could make Shaun feel like she was on his side, maybe she could get out of this mess alive.

"And it's not fair," Lacey said. "You feel like you're owed something, because you are. You're owed your mother's love. But you can never have it. So you want the next best thing. Her painting."

For a brief second, it looked like Shaun was going to relent. But then his dark eyes flashed with menace.

"Why should I listen to anyone who was friends with *them*?" he challenged. "Any friend of my mother's and her garbage husband is an enemy of me!"

Lacey grimaced at Shaun's disparaging comment, at his complete disregard for human life. She was losing him again.

"I'm not friends with them," Lacey said, desperately. "I barely knew Edwin. I got wrapped up in all of this by accident."

"I don't believe you," Shaun said, glowering at Lacey. "You have my painting." He raised the hammer. "And I have ways of making you talk."

It was too late. Lacey's attempts to get on his side had failed. There was only one thing left to do.

Moving at lightning speed, Lacey kicked out with both feet, getting Shaun square in the stomach.

He staggered back, looking shocked, and slammed into the mantelpiece over the fireplace. As he sunk to the floor, dazed, Lacey took the split-second reprieve to leap off the couch.

She ran for her life.

CHAPTER THIRTY FIVE

Lacey's heart pounded in her throat as she dashed out of the living room and beelined for the kitchen.

She heard thudding coming from behind. She looked back. Shaun was staggering out of the living room door, dazed. He was holding his hammer.

"Chester!" Lacey cried.

Immediately at her command, the dog came springing out through the kitchen door.

He passed her in a blur of fur and launched himself through the air just as Shaun reached the threshold of the kitchen.

From behind, Lacey heard Shaun let out a roar of pain. As she slammed the kitchen door behind her, she caught a glimpse of Chester with his jaws latched around the man's ankle, and Shaun's eyes shooting daggers into her.

The horrible image seared into Lacey's mind as she streaked across the kitchen to the stable-style back door. She grabbed the bottom lock, which she'd fastened so securely earlier, and tried to wiggle the rusted bolt open. But it was stuck in place, refusing to maneuver. She abandoned it and tried the top one. She could jump if she had to. But to her horror, Lacey discovered it, too, was stuck in place. She'd never had cause to use the deadbolts before, and now they were in place, they were refusing to budge.

Coming from the corridor came the sounds of Chester snarling, and a horrible thudding sound that must be Shaun's hammer slamming into the walls. Lacey couldn't even bear to picture the danger Chester was in right now. Her fearless dog was risking his life for her. If anything happened to him...

Lacey shook the thought off immediately. Right now, she had to focus on escaping. She had to find another exit. Her gaze went straight to the window above the kitchen sink.

She darted for it, climbing up on the counter and flinging it open.

"Call the police!" she screamed into the blackness, as she began to clamber out of it.

If Gina was home, she'd hear her. But it looked like all the lights were out in Gina's house. Lacey was alone up on the cliffside with a deranged killer and no one to help.

Suddenly, Lacey felt hands tighten around her leg. She glanced back. Shaun had grabbed hold of her. His pant leg was soaked with blood, and he'd left a trail on the kitchen floor behind him.

Lacey tried to kick back at him, but he was expecting it and dodged.

Suddenly, Lacey felt herself being tugged backward through the window she was half hanging out of. She fell back off the counter and slammed onto the floor.

Shaun towered above her, hammer raised.

"Give me the painting!" he screamed. "Or I'll break your legs!"

Lacey had a horrible image of this being what Edwin was confronted with in his final moments. Torture. But unlike her, Edwin had known all along where he'd hidden the painting. He'd sacrificed his life in order to guard Diane's secret.

Suddenly, Chester came charging at Shaun and leapt for his chest. Shaun staggered back into the kitchen sink.

Then Lacey saw him. Tom! He was climbing in through the kitchen window.

Lacey had no time to process what was happening. She left Tom to tackle Shaun and grabbed her phone, punching in *9-9-9*.

"Home invasion!" she screamed. "Crag Cottage! He has a hammer!"

Then she dropped the phone and ran back into the kitchen.

Shaun and Tom were grappling on the kitchen floor. Tom was the bigger and fitter of the two, but Shaun had the advantage of murderous adrenaline and nothing left to lose to fuel him.

There was only one option. Lacey had to subdue Shaun. It was the only way.

She grabbed the closest heavy object—her favorite Le Creuset casserole dish—and brought it crashing down on Shaun's head.

Like a lightbulb going out, Shaun stopped fighting. He flopped limply on top of Tom, pinning him to the ground like a sleeping giant. He was out like a light.

From his squashed position on the floor, Tom looked over at Lacey, his face red from effort. He blew his messed up, sweat-streaked hair from his face.

"Sorry I'm late," he quipped.

CHAPTER THIRTY SIX

The police arrived at Crag Cottage in a flurry of flashing lights and sirens. Before Lacey knew it, her home was overrun.

She panted, trying to catch her breath, as what felt like a thousand people swarmed into her kitchen, heavy boots thundering on the floorboards. And there, bringing up the rear, was Beth Lewis.

She gave her a single nod, before walking up to Shaun and cuffing him.

"You're being arrested for assault," she told Shaun.

She heaved him to his feet and marched him out the front door.

Lacey collected herself. Her heart was thrumming, and her body hurt all over from being tackled to the ground.

One of the officers approached her for her statement. While she spoke, a cop bagged up the hammer Shaun had left behind.

"We should get you to hospital," the cop told Lacey. "Get you checked over."

Lacey shook her head. "I'm fine. What about Tom? Chester?"

Just then, the kitchen door opened. Chester rushed her, running circles around her. She patted him as Tom strode up to her and pulled her into his arms.

"You're okay," Lacey said, sighing her relief into Tom's chest.

Now she understood what Tom had meant when he'd said he'd hate anything to happen to her.

"We're okay," he echoed, kissing her.

Lacey heard footsteps behind, and Tom's arms loosened. She looked over to see Superintendent Turner waltz into her kitchen like he owned the place.

"Good job, boys," he said to the cops, triumphantly.

The two female officers in attendance caught one another's eye, looking unimpressed.

Just then, DCI Lewis reentered the kitchen and looked at her superintendent.

"I think you'll find Lacey is the one due the credit," she said.

Superintendent Turner froze. He glowered as he looked over at Lacey. He let out a begrudging nod.

"Thanks for your help on this matter," he said, tightly.

From behind him, Lacey noticed Beth smirking.

As the cops continued their work securing the scene, the female detective approached Lacey. Lacey swallowed nervously. They still hadn't patched things up from before, and she wasn't sure how Beth would feel about it all.

"Lacey," she said with a nod. "Excellent job."

Lacey widened her eyes. "You mean that?"

"I do," Beth said. "You solved it, Lacey. I'm sure it won't provide much comfort considering the circumstances, but thanks to you, Edwin's murder has been solved."

If Lacey hadn't been in such a state, she would have felt vindicated. But as it stood, she was still reeling from Shaun's revelations to celebrate.

"He confessed," Lacey said, her heart heavy. "He told me everything. About how he killed Edwin. Why."

Beth nodded reassuringly. "Don't worry. We've got this in hand. We've arrested him for assaulting you, but he'll be charged with murdering Edwin once we're done with questioning him."

"Does this mean I'm forgiven now?" Lacey asked Beth.

"I'm grateful you cracked the case," Beth said. "Let's leave it at that for now."

"That's good enough for me," Lacey said.

Beth joined the rest of her team, and Chester started fussing around Lacey's legs, demanding his share of attention.

"Who's my furry hero?" Lacey said, ruffling his fur behind the ears. She looked up at Tom. "And my other hero. Excellent window-climbing work."

"All that mountain climbing and abseiling came in handy after all," Tom joked.

Lacey embraced him, beyond relieved they were all still in one piece.

"Hey, I just thought," Tom said. "What ever happened to the painting? The one Shaun was looking for? You don't have it. It wasn't at Chumley's, either. So where is it?"

It was the final mystery left to solve.

"I told Edwin to reframe it again," Lacey said. "Behind a painting like how it was when I found it. I guess he hid it really, really well."

Just then, her gaze fell to the red streak on her floorboards. She was hit by a sudden thought.

"I have an idea!" she exclaimed, pulling out of Tom's arms.

She hurried over to DCI Lewis.

"Beth, did Edwin have paint on his hands?" she asked. "When they found his body?"

Beth looked spooked. "Yes...Why?"

"Was it red?"

Now Beth looked totally spooked. "Who told you that?"

"No one," Lacey said.

She had a hunch about where the painting was hidden. Now to see if it was right.

CHAPTER THIRTY SEVEN

"Thanks for meeting me here," Lacey said, as Bryan Vallins stopped beside her, outside the humble bungalow cottage that was Edwin and Diane Cross's former home.

It had been nearly impossible to find the place. It was situated down a country road so obscured by overgrown hedgerows it was nearly impossible to see it. It definitely wasn't the sort of place you could accidentally stumble across. Only someone with a very good knowledge of the local geography would ever be able to find it. Good thing Shaun hadn't got there first. The story may well have had a very different outcome if he had.

It was the morning after the attack. As soon as the police had vacated her property, Lacey had called Bryan with her idea about where Edwin may have hidden the painting.

Superintendent Turner had said they'd looked behind all the paintings at Chumley's. But he'd never said anything about Edwin's home....

"It's good to see you, Lacey," Bryan said, leaning down to give Chester a greeting pat. "I'm glad you called. I have some news."

"Oh?" Lacey asked.

She suspected it had something to do with Shaun's arrest.

"Someone's been arrested for Edwin's murder," he announce. "Shaun Milton. He's a Devon Gas engineer, who apparently used his credentials to trick people into letting him inside their homes to rob them."

Lacey held her tongue. Bryan didn't need to know she'd been instrumental in Shaun's arrest. In fact, the less he knew about her involvement the better. It was the only way she could be certain to keep Diane's secret.

"That's good news," Lacey said. "I hope he confesses so you and Joy don't have to go through a court case."

Bryan nodded his thanks, though he looked far from happy.

It was a bittersweet moment, Lacey understood. There were no winners in a situation like this.

"Shall we go and look for this painting then?" Bryan said.

170

Lacey nodded, feeling nervous with apprehension.

Bryan removed a set of keys from his pocket and unlocked the door of the cottage, then gestured Lacey inside.

She entered, Chester in tow, and glanced around.

The small, modest home was exactly what she'd expected from a man like Edwin Cross. Homely and comfortable. Every spare inch of the walls was adorned with a photograph of his late wife and their two best friends, Joy and Bryan. It was a touching tribute, and a testament to what mattered to Edwin. He'd lived a simple, quiet life with the woman he'd waited forty years to marry.

Lacey tried to take comfort in the words of Bryan's obituary; Diane and Edwin were reunited now. Back together, as they always were meant to be. Lacey knew Edwin would forgive Diane for hiding the truth about Shaun from him. He would understand why she'd done what she had. They would be together now, at peace, living the quiet life they deserved.

"What is it we're looking for?" Bryan asked.

Just then, Lacey spotted something. Above the mantelpiece was a painting of a bowl of tomatoes. It was similar enough to the one she'd purchased from Edwin for her to know it had been painted by Edwin's hand. The colors were bright enough to show it had only very recently been hung.

"That," Lacey said, pointing at the tomato painting, a small smile twitching at the corners of her lips.

Carefully, she removed the painting from its hook and laid it across the coffee table. She prized away the back panel.

There it was.

The self-portrait of Diane Cross painted under the pseudonym of Carson Desi.

Bryan gasped. Tears flooded his eyes.

"How did you know it would be here?" he asked, sounding astounded.

"It's an in-joke," Lacey told him.

Just then, she noticed something else wedged in the frame of the painting. It looked like an envelope.

She frowned and picked it up. To her surprise, the letter was addressed to her.

Bryan's eyebrows rose with astonishment. "What is that?"

"No idea," Lacey said, as she quickly opened the envelope and unfolded the paper inside.

She read aloud.

"Dear Lacey,

"Thank you for returning my wife's portrait to me. It was her wish to have all her paintings donated after her death, but I couldn't quite bear to part with this one. When I finally decided to fulfil Diane's wishes, I hid it behind the painting you bought. But I deeply regretted it. So you can imagine my surprise when it came right back to me, the very next day! Perhaps I'm foolish to think it was fate. Perhaps it's silly to think it was a sign that Diane was watching me from above. Whatever reason the world saw fit to return it to me, I'm glad they did.

"If you're reading this letter, I can only presume it means I have now passed away, and the tomato painting, which I have left to you in my will, has found its way to your hands, and your curiosity has compelled you to check behind it just in case. Well congratulations! I hope you enjoy your prize. Diane and I loved to play practical jokes and tricks on one another, and I hope this gives us both a chuckle as we watch over you from above."

The words became blurry as tears flooded into Lacey's eyes. She couldn't believe it, and choked up. Edwin had written this letter with no idea he would be killed the next day. He'd never even had a chance to get her added to his will, so the tomato painting would never have reached her through legal means as he'd intended.

"Aren't you going to read the P.S.?" Bryan asked.

Lacey hadn't even noticed it. She wiped the tears from her eyes and turned the letter over.

"P.S. I know my store is mainly full of bric-a-brac, but I hope you can find something of worth in Chumley's, since the store is now yours."

Now the tears spilled from her eyes in earnest. Lacey couldn't believe it. It was too much to take in in one go. Hearing Edwin speak to her from the grave made her grief for him even stronger. Knowing he cared about her so much after just that one gesture of her returning the painting of his beloved wife was just too much to comprehend.

Bryan squeezed her shoulder. "Looks like he wanted the painting to go to you."

Lacey shook her head. Bryan deserved to keep it. He'd cried when he saw it. It obviously meant so much to him.

"I can't accept it," she said. "Not the painting, or the store. It's yours. Edwin wrote this letter thinking it would be read years and years from now, when you'd all passed."

"Who cares about that," Bryan said. "In the end, you're the one he wanted to inherit it."

"But..." she began.

"I don't want an antiques store," Bryan assured her. "Neither does Joy! Edwin left us this bungalow and that's plenty for us. Joy's going to turn it into a rescue dog sanctuary."

"Then sell the painting and use the proceeds to fund it," Lacey pleaded.

Bryan shook his head. He was as stubborn as Edwin had been when she'd tried to return the painting the first time around.

Suddenly, Lacey hit on a thought.

"I know," she said. "I have a compromise. The same one I made with Edwin in the first place. One that will keep Edwin and Diane's joke alive."

"Oh?" Bryan asked, looking curious.

Lacey handed the frame and both paintings to Bryan. "Reframe it. Keep the painting hidden beneath. Hang it up in your dog sanctuary on proud display. Who knows, maybe the *Wilfordshire Weekly* will do a piece on you guys and your new dog sanctuary, and it can be there behind you in the photo, just like it was with Edwin all those years ago."

Bryan's eyes started to mist over. It was clear he was touched by Lacey's idea.

"All right," he said, finally. "You twisted my arm. I'll hide the painting somewhere only you will know of. And when the time comes, and Joy and I pass, it will come back to you, just like Edwin wanted."

Lacey held her hand out to shake his. "It's a deal."

EPILOGUE

"Lacey!" Tom called. "Come and look at this!"

Lacey put down the teapot she'd been inspecting and picked her way through the crowded aisles of Chumley's antiques store. She found Tom surrounded by toys.

"I found two more Scalextric sets!" he said, beaming up at her.

Lacey smiled with contentment.

After everything that happened with Edwin, she'd learned something very important. Your first go at life was bound to go wrong. All the decisions you'd made were when you were a completely different person, after all, with different goals, and a different outlook on life. It took time to find out what you wanted, and who you were, and who you wanted to achieve all those things with. It took guts to realize that and seek out a new life, but it was never too late.

Just like Diane and Edwin, Lacey's truth had been there all along. And like Diane and Edwin, it had taken her forty years to accept it and take the plunge. For Edwin and Diane, they'd realized they loved one another and wanted to live a quiet life together. For Lacey, it had taken accepting that she was her father's daughter through and through, that she couldn't force herself into a corporate life in New York City when her soul was crying out for antiques and craggy cliffs beside the ocean.

"I've made a decision," Lacey suddenly announced.

Curiosity twinkled in Tom's green eyes. "About what?"

"The wedding."

Tom's eyebrows inched up with surprise. "Oh?"

"I know what season I want to get married in. Winter. I want a winter wedding."

Tom looked surprised. "Really? I thought for sure you'd pick next fall. But I guess if you want a little more time to prepare, that makes sense."

Lacey started to chuckle. "Not next winter. This winter."

Tom looked stunned. "*This* winter? As in... *THIS WINTER?*"

Lacey laughed and nodded. "This winter! I don't want to wait forever to start my second life with you. I want to start it now. As soon as possible."

174

Tom's face cracked into a grin. He swirled her up in his arms and kissed her. Then he set her down on her feet.

"I've got so much to prepare," he suddenly exclaimed. "The gingerbread igloo. The macaron Santa."

He laughed. "Only kidding."

Lacey gave him a playful nudge. "We'd better tell my mom before anyone else. You up for a video call?"

"You bet!" Tom said.

Lacey smiled. This was how they should've announced their engagement in the first place. A video call to her family in New York.

They shoved aside some bric-a-brac they'd piled up on a purple velvet couch and sat side by side. Lacey perched the laptop on her knees.

When the call connected, Lacey was happy to see Naomi and Frankie happened to be at Shirley's apartment. Perfect. She could tell them all at the same time.

"Where are you?" Shirley asked, frowning at the grubby purple couch.

"My new store," Lacey told her.

Lacey watched as her mom, sister, and nephew bunched together on the screen, exchanging confused looks. She smiled.

"You bought a new store?" Naomi asked.

"Not quite," Lacey replied. "I was bequeathed one."

"Bequeathed?" Naomi echoed. "What does that mean?"

"It just means someone left it to her in their will when they died," her intelligent ginger son explained. "Who died, Auntie Lacey?"

"A friend," Lacey replied, wistfully, remembering Edwin. "A good friend."

"Is that why you're calling?" Naomi asked, looking perplexed. "To tell us you got given a gross couch by some old dude?"

Tactless as ever, Lacey thought.

"Actually, no," she said aloud. "We called because we have news."

"You're pregnant," Shirley said, with a gasp.

"No!" Lacey exclaimed. "We know when we want to get married." She took a breath. "Winter. This winter."

Her mom's eyes widened with shock.

"That's very soon!" she cried.

Lacey nodded, feeling herself grinning from ear to ear.

175

"Can it be after Christmas?" Naomi asked. "You know Christmas flights cost the earth, and Frankie doesn't start back at school until the tenth."

Shirley grabbed her diary and perched it on her knees. "I'd prefer the seventh."

Lacey looked at Tom adoringly. "How does January seventh sound for you?"

He squeezed her hand. "It sounds perfect."

Lacey turned back to the screen. "The seventh it is."

*

"We have news," Lacey announced joyfully, as she entered the store hand in hand with Tom.

Then suddenly, a cold blast of air hit her. She shivered.

Finnbar and Gina looked over from where they were arranging stock on a shelf. They were both wearing gloves, scarves, and thick coats.

"What's going on?" Lacey asked, bemused.

Gina answered. "Th—the air conditioning."

She pointed a gloved finger at the newly installed system in the wall between Lacey's antiques store and the boutique. It was juddering away, unnecessarily blasting frigid air into the store. Typical that the thing would be up and running just in time for the change in weather.

"Does anyone know how to turn it off?" Lacey asked.

"T—Taryn," Finnbar said through chattering teeth. "Left the manual on the c—counter."

The arctic air swirled around Lacey as she headed to the counter to retrieve the instruction manual. But like most technology stuff, it seemed like gobbledygook to her.

"Tom? Can you?" she asked.

So much for a surprise announcement. Taryn's blasted AC unit had put a damper on that!

As Tom began fiddling with the controls, pressing buttons and making it bleep and whirr, Lacey heard the bell go. She looked up. It was Taryn.

"YOU!" Lacey said before the fashionista got a chance to get a word in edgewise.

Taryn paused and raised an eyebrow of surprise. She folded her arms defensively. Lacey noticed she was holding the bill in her hand.

176

"I'm not paying that," Lacey told her. "You did all this work without my permission, and I don't even know how to work the damn thing. And have you been taking my mail? I haven't had a scrap of mail for weeks!"

Taryn's expression turned pinched. "Actually, I was coming to tell you the workman was a crook. All the hot air from your store is blowing into mine. So I'm going to have to get the unit removed again. I'll pay, obviously. And… I'm sorry."

Lacey was stunned. She'd never heard Taryn say sorry for any of the annoying, petty things she'd done. It was satisfying to see her with her tail between her legs, for once. Lacey would be forgiven for wanting to rub it in her face, but she wasn't that cruel.

"I'm sorry it didn't pan out how you expected," Lacey told her. "It's never nice to be scammed."

Taryn smiled thinly. She turned to leave, but paused and looked back. "Oh. And I didn't take your mail. I've no idea what that was about."

She left. Lacey stood pondering in the middle of her store.

"Erm… Lacey?" came Finnbar's voice.

She looked over. His timid posture made him seem even shorter than usual.

"What is it?" she asked. This clearly wasn't going anywhere good.

Before Finnbar had a chance to answer, Gina bustled over.

"What was your news?" she asked, interrupting whatever Finnbar was about to say.

He slunk back, as if giving her the floor.

"My news," Lacey said. She looked at Tom. "*Our* news."

Tom stopped fiddling with the AC unit controller and joined her by her side, wrapping an arm around her shoulder.

"What?" Gina asked excitedly.

"We've set the date for the wedding," Tom said.

"January seventh," Lacey added.

Gina looked panicked. "This January seventh? The one coming up?"

Lacey nodded. "Yup."

"But I didn't think you wanted a winter wedding!" Gina cried. "I haven't even looked at winter flowers. And now you're giving me less than four months' notice?"

"You can do it, Gina," Lacey said. "I have faith."

"Congratulations, Lacey," Finnbar said, in his awkward and stilted way.

Lacey felt pretty bad for everything she'd put him through. The poor boy was just trying to earn a bit of cash to support his studies, and she'd gotten him embroiled in a murder case, pointed the finger of suspicion at him, and still he'd come back to work for her. He was indeed a curious fellow, because his capacity to forgive belied anyone she'd ever met. They were going to get on just fine, she decided.

Then Finnbar handed her a stack of letters on the counter. A very thick stack.

"Er, Finnbar, what is that?" she asked.

"Your mail," her employee squeaked in a small, guilty voice. "We got a new postman and he was doing a different route so was delivering it at midday. Since you guys were always out on lunch, I started piling it up. And I totally forgot to tell you about it."

Lacey couldn't believe it. All that time she'd been wondering why she wasn't getting any mail, and Finnbar had been squirreling it away the whole time.

She took the bundles and began leafing through. It was mainly bills, but the stack was interspersed by colorful envelopes no doubt containing cards of congratulations. Lacey thumbed through them, seeing how many had postage stamps from the States. She winced at the thought of all her distant cousins and aunts back home who'd gone out of their way (and shelled out for the extortionate postage fee) to send her and Tom their well wishes on their engagement. They must all be wondering when she'd become so rude that she didn't even thank them for their cards!

Just then, Lacey noticed something that made her pause. Among all the colorful envelopes postmarked in the US, there was a plain white one with a UK stamp mark on it. Not just UK, but Sussex, UK.

Her heart stopped.

She stared at it, at the address, at the handwriting that was suddenly so familiar to her.

"Tom…" she gasped, going cold all over. "My dad got my letter." She held up the envelope. "And he wrote me one back."

NOW AVAILABLE!

SILENCED BY A SPELL
(A Lacey Doyle Cozy Mystery—Book 7)

"Very entertaining. I highly recommend this book to the permanent library of any reader that appreciates a very well written mystery, with some twists and an intelligent plot. You will not be disappointed. Excellent way to spend a cold weekend!" --Books and Movie Reviews, Roberto Mattos (regarding *Murder in the Manor*)

SILENCED BY A SPELL (A LACEY DOYLE COZY MYSTERY— BOOK 7) is book seven in a charming new cozy mystery series which begins with MURDER IN THE MANOR (Book #1), a #1 Bestseller with over 100 five-star reviews—and a free download!

Lacey Doyle, 39 years old and freshly divorced, has made a drastic change: she has walked away from the fast life of New York City and settled down in the quaint English seaside town of Wilfordshire.

With Halloween fast approaching, Lacey lucks out when she's given a rare, ancient book that's perfect for her upcoming spooky auction. But after the book is sold to a buyer, the mysterious book vanishes before she can deliver it. Even stranger, the equally mysterious seller has disappeared—just as a body turns up dead.

With her reputation on the line, Lacey finds herself in the fight of her life to save her business and clear her name—and, with the help of her beloved dog, to solve the mysterious disappearance.

FRAMED BY A FORGERY (Book #8), and CATASTROPHE IN A CLOISTER (Book #9) are also available!

Fiona Grace

Debut author Fiona Grace is author of the LACEY DOYLE COZY MYSTERY series, comprising nine books (and counting); of the TUSCAN VINEYARD COZY MYSTERY series, comprising six books (and counting); of the DUBIOUS WITCH COZY MYSTERY series, comprising three books (and counting); of the BEACHFRONT BAKERY COZY MYSTERY series, comprising six books (and counting); and of the CATS AND DOGS COZY MYSTERY series, comprising three books (and counting).

Fiona would love to hear from you, so please visit www.fionagraceauthor.com to receive free ebooks, hear the latest news, and stay in touch.

BOOKS BY FIONA GRACE

LACEY DOYLE COZY MYSTERY
MURDER IN THE MANOR (Book#1)
DEATH AND A DOG (Book #2)
CRIME IN THE CAFE (Book #3)
VEXED ON A VISIT (Book #4)
KILLED WITH A KISS (Book #5)
PERISHED BY A PAINTING (Book #6)
SILENCED BY A SPELL (Book #7)
FRAMED BY A FORGERY (Book #8)
CATASTROPHE IN A CLOISTER (Book #9)

TUSCAN VINEYARD COZY MYSTERY
AGED FOR MURDER (Book #1)
AGED FOR DEATH (Book #2)
AGED FOR MAYHEM (Book #3)
AGED FOR SEDUCTION (Book #4)
AGED FOR VENGEANCE (Book #5)
AGED FOR ACRIMONY (Book #6)

DUBIOUS WITCH COZY MYSTERY
SKEPTIC IN SALEM: AN EPISODE OF MURDER (Book #1)
SKEPTIC IN SALEM: AN EPISODE OF CRIME (Book #2)
SKEPTIC IN SALEM: AN EPISODE OF DEATH (Book #3)

BEACHFRONT BAKERY COZY MYSTERY
BEACHFRONT BAKERY: A KILLER CUPCAKE (Book #1)
BEACHFRONT BAKERY: A MURDEROUS MACARON (Book #2)
BEACHFRONT BAKERY: A PERILOUS CAKE POP (Book #3)
BEACHFRONT BAKERY: A DEADLY DANISH (Book #4)
BEACHFRONT BAKERY: A TREACHEROUS TART (Book #5)
BEACHFRONT BAKERY: A CALAMITOUS COOKIE (Book #6)

CATS AND DOGS COZY MYSTERY
A VILLA IN SICILY: OLIVE OIL AND MURDER (Book #1)
A VILLA IN SICILY: FIGS AND A CADAVER (Book #2)
A VILLA IN SICILY: VINO AND DEATH (Book #3)